A/R R.L. 5.4 Pts. 7

D0450106

DISCARD Liberty Lake Municipal Library

Please do not attempt to repair
damages. Alert the library

······························

Snow in Summer

······························

PHILOMEL BOOKS

A division of Penguin Young Readers Group.
Published by The Penguin Group.
Penguin Group (USA) Inc., 375 Hudson Street, New York, NY 10014, U.S.A.
Penguin Group (Canada), 90 Eglinton Avenue East, Suite 700, Toronto,
Ontario M4P 2Y3, Canada (a division of Pearson Penguin Canada Inc.).
Penguin Books Ltd, 80 Strand, London WC2R 0RL, England.
Penguin Ireland, 25 St. Stephen's Green, Dublin 2,
Ireland (a division of Penguin Books Ltd).
Penguin Group (Australia), 250 Camberwell Road, Camberwell, Victoria
3124, Australia (a division of Pearson Australia Group Pty Ltd).
Penguin Books India Pvt Ltd, 11 Community Centre,
Panchsheel Park, New Delhi—110 017, India.
Penguin Group (NZ), 67 Apollo Drive, Rosedale, Auckland 0632,
New Zealand (a division of Pearson New Zealand Ltd).
Penguin Books (South Africa) (Pty) Ltd, 24 Sturdee Avenue,
Rosebank, Johannesburg 2196, South Africa. Penguin Books Ltd,
Registered Offices: 80 Strand, London WC2R 0RL, England.

Copyright © 2011 by Jane Yolen. All rights reserved.
This book, or parts thereof, may not be reproduced in any form without permission
in writing from the publisher, Philomel Books, a division of Penguin Young Readers Group,
345 Hudson Street, New York, NY 10014. Philomel Books, Reg. U.S. Pat. & Tm. Off.
The scanning, uploading and distribution of this book via the Internet or via any other
means without the permission of the publisher is illegal and punishable by law.
Please purchase only authorized electronic editions, and do not participate in or encourage
electronic piracy of copyrighted materials. Your support of the author's rights is appreciated.
The publisher does not have any control over and does not assume any responsibility
for author or third-party websites or their content. Published simultaneously in Canada.
Printed in the United States of America. Edited by Jill Santopolo. Design by Amy Wu.
Text set in 11.5 point Adobe Caslon.

Library of Congress Cataloging-in-Publication Data
Yolen, Jane.   Snow in Summer / Jane Yolen.   p. cm.
Summary: Recasts the tale of Snow White, setting it in West
Virginia in the 1940s with a stepmother who is a snake-handler.
[1. Fairy tales. 2. Stepmothers—Fiction. 3. Magic—Fiction.
4. West Virginia—History—20th century—Fiction.] I. Title.
PZ8.Y78Sn 2011   [Fic]—dc22   2010044242

ISBN 978-0-399-25663-9
1 3 5 7 9 10 8 6 4 2

Fairest of Them All

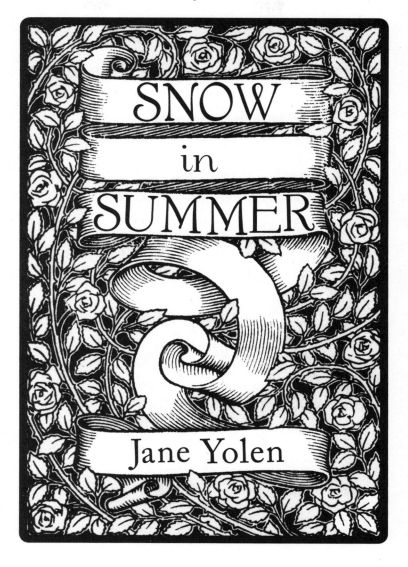

SNOW
in
SUMMER

Jane Yolen

PHILOMEL BOOKS
An Imprint of Penguin Group (USA) Inc.

DISCARD

ALSO BY THE SAME AUTHOR:

The Devil's Arithmetic

Queen's Own Fool

Girl in a Cage

Except the Queen

Prince Across the Water

The Rogues

The Sea Man

Children of the Wolf

· · · · · · · ·

To editor Jill Santopolo, who asked for this;
to my daughter, Heidi Stemple, for the use of her birthday;
to beta reader Debby Harris for plot conversations
and good revision notes; to my beloved Webster County,
West Virginia, in-laws for fiddly stuff; to my agent,
Elizabeth Harding, for years of cheerleading;
to my writers' group for encouragement; and to all the
Facebook friends who sent me information about cauls.

I read three books on snake-handling sects,
which told me more than I wanted to know about that
particular phenomenon: Dennis Covington's *Salvation
on Sand Mountain,* Thomas Burton's *Serpent-Handling
Believers,* and Fred Brown and Jeanne McDonald's
The Serpent Handlers: Three Families and Their Faith.

ACKNOWLEDGMENT
My short story "Snow in Summer," © 2000,
first published in Ellen Datlow and Terri
Windling's anthology *Black Hearts, Ivory Bones.*
It has served as the basis for this novel.

Liberty Lake Municipal Library
Washington

Please do not attempt to repair
damages. Alert the library

AUTHOR'S NOTE

Addison, aka Webster Springs, West Virginia, is a real Webster County town on the Elk River. Nineteenth-century visitors flooded there to take the waters of the salt sulfur springs. My husband and his three brothers were all born and brought up there, and we spent a number of vacations in Webster Springs and at their cabin at Camp Caesar. Their mother and father gave the land behind their brick house to build the first Catholic church in town in the 1940s. I have put gemstone mining in the mountain region east of Webster though much of that was actually done in and around Seneca Rocks.

The real Addison/Webster Springs has nothing at all to do with this story and the deplorable and magical events that happen in this book. They exist only in the author's imagination, as do the folk herein, though I have borrowed local names, and for that I thank the good people of Webster Springs, friends and classmates of my late husband, David Stemple.

"Memory isn't just mutable, it's associative."

—MIRA BARTÓK, *The Memory Palace*

PHOTOGRAPH

have an old black-and-white photograph on my wall of all the things Papa loved. Its edges are curling and brown. In those days in the small towns of West Virginia, we didn't have cameras that could take a picture in color. I've no idea who took that photograph, but I do know how it came into my hands. Cousin Nancy gave it to me years after this story happened.

· · · · · · ·

1

Long after.

In the photograph, the mountains stand side by side, stiff and unyielding, like brothers who have given up talking to one another. Those mountains hold bears and coon, turkeys and partridge, as well as squirrels and greasy groundhogs that all made fine eating. "Nature's larder," Papa called it. These days, though, what with strip mining and clear-cutting of trees, nothing is like it was then. There's some good in that—and a lot of not-so-good, too.

The picture was taken right before Christmas, and the snow stands knee-deep on the mountainsides. Knee-deep, that is, for a man. For a seven-year-old, it's much higher.

Staring straight ahead, Papa is walking along the wintry track, oblivious to the softly falling snow or the girl beside him, reaching out to touch his cold fingers. She is awkward in her new dark blue coat and hat, unused to such finery, and has one booted foot held high to step over the snow.

Striding along on the other side of the child is Cousin Nancy, who'd been at school with Papa and married his cousin Jack. She'd been best friends with Mama. A recent war widow, she's a woman with a kind face and kinder heart—though one cannot quite get that from the picture. Her best features are her eyes, the color of water rushing down a mountain stream, green and gray. She's the one holding my right hand, warming it in hers.

Behind us comes a long line of our neighbors, somber as their clothes. They stare ahead as if what is to come is at least as awful as what is behind. These are the folk who had known me since before I was born. Some of them even knew Papa before he was born. Kinfolk if not particular kind folk. The ones who sit on the front porch and gossip. Storying, they call it. Our lives and our stories entwined.

Ahead of us is a flatbed cart, drawn by four big black horses with crow feathers twisted in their manes. Barrel-chested and heavy-legged, they're being led along the track by Preacher Watson, his tall black hat spotted by the snow. We're a sorry congregation, walking in the horses' hoof-prints or the ruts made by the wheels of the cart. All the way up to the old cemetery where all us Mortons get buried—spring, summer, fall, or winter—the cemetery next to the old church, where only owls and crows worship now.

On the flatbed, in a pine box, lies Mama, cold and distant, who had always been warm and welcoming, with the dead baby in her arms. She's wearing her wedding dress, white silk with a scattering of lace. I knew that, because I kissed her before the box's top was nailed down. I didn't kiss the baby. I hadn't known him all that long. Just three

· · · · · · · ·

days. Long enough for him to be baptized, long enough for him to die in Mama's arms, long enough for Mama to be dead beside him. Papa took his picture after he'd died and kept that picture propped up on the mantel for some time: a thin, dead baby in a long white christening gown. The one I'd worn when I was an infant. The one he was buried in.

There are tears like black stains running down my cheeks for I must have rubbed my eyes many times in the long walk up the mountain. It looks as if the crow feathers had been used to paint streaks under my eyes. There are no tear stains on Papa's face. If there are any on Cousin Nancy's, I can't tell for she is not looking up at the camera but down at me.

In that photograph, on that mountain ridge, heading toward the graveyard, were all the things Papa loved then.

And later.

·1·

SNOW IN SUMMER

he town of Addison lies between two high mountains. Those mountains were cut through by the Elk River many hundreds of thousands of years ago, and all that was left was a little bit of bottomland. But it was a fertile place. Everything you could ever want to grow there grew heartily: beans, cabbage, turnips, potatoes, greens, corn, squash as big as pumpkins. Even if you didn't

have a green thumb, *something* could grow. But if you had garden magic at your fingertips, life in Addison was a pleasant place indeed.

My grandpap five times removed had that green magic. He'd come over from Scotland and said that Addison reminded him of the mountains there. Of course, Grandpap was gone a long time before I was ever born, and I only know the stories.

I'd been born on July 1, 1937, ten pounds of squalling baby, with a full head of black hair. It was a hard birth that nearly killed Mama. Though the next baby, being even bigger, actually did.

Cousin Nancy, who'd been there to help with my birthing, told me all about it later, after Mama died. "White caul, black hair, and all that blood," she said.

I shuddered at the blood part, but Cousin Nancy explained it was good blood, not bad.

"Not like later," I said, meaning when Mama died, and Cousin Nancy nodded because nothing more needed to be added.

It was my ninth birthday when she told me the story. We were sitting on the old divan in her front parlor, the parlor that also served as the town's post office, in the only brick house on Main Street. I was scrunched up next to

· · · · · · · ·

her, my feet tucked under my bottom. She was in her black rayon silk print with its smattering of pink flowers and green leaves. She'd had it for as long as I could remember. Her hair was done up in braids across the top of her head like a crown because it was such a hot summer day. One long tendril had escaped.

She was showing me the photo album she'd rescued when Papa wanted to bury it with Mama and the baby.

"I looked your papa square in the eye," she said, her right pointy finger raised. "Told him straight out, 'You got one living child, Lem, and she'll want to know her mama someday.'" She shook that finger at me as if I was Papa. Cousin Nancy rarely snaps at anyone, though she always looks them square in the eye, so I guess Papa listened up because there was the photo album in her lap.

Cousin Nancy showed me that album twice a year, on my birthday, as she was the only one who remembered when that was, and on Christmas. "We got to keep that album neat and clean, 'cause it's all you've got left of your mama," she told me. So I always had to wash my hands to handle it, with the little pink soap she kept in her bathroom that smelled of roses.

That was also the day she told me that I'd been born with the white caul over my head, like a little helmet. I

· · · · · · · ·

know now that a caul is the membrane, a see-through bit of skin that some babies are born with over their heads and faces, but I didn't know it then.

"Caul?" I said it as if it was the word *cold*. "But it was July." There was a fan wheezing overhead trying to keep us cool, and failing.

She pronounced it for me again. We both loved odd words. "You're one of the veil born, child." She made a sign with her hand, the one with the two outside fingers standing up, like horns to ward off any evil. "Destined for greatness. You'll be able to see dead folk. Least, that's what *my* auntie told me, and she was born with a caul herself."

"I want to see *Mama*," I whispered. Mama had been dead almost two years at that time, short enough for the ache to still run deep, long enough so I'd already begun to forget her. I understood about death, knew I wasn't going to see her again. Not then at any rate. Not for a long time. Not till heaven.

But the sad fact was that there were some days I hardly remembered Mama. Sometimes I even believed Cousin Nancy was my mama. My *other* mama. Even though she didn't live with Papa and me. After all, she was the one who fed me and bathed me. She was the one who brushed out and plaited my long dark hair each day before I went to school. And while Papa still occasionally told me stories

• • • • • • • •

8

when I went to bed, or looked over my homework, Cousin Nancy always came to our house before dawn so Papa could go out to work in the fields. She came just to make sure I was properly turned out for school and then went back to her own house to open up the post office.

I think that day I said I wanted to see Mama because Cousin Nancy wanted me to. She was my godmother and I tried to please *her* since I couldn't seem to please Papa, who felt as far away as Mama, only not shut away in a box.

Cousin Nancy quickly told me the rest of the story about my birth, guessing how the story was gonna make me forget my troubles. And hers. She recalled that while Mama was birthing me, Papa was out in the garden throwing up.

"Throwing up!" I couldn't quite believe it.

She put her arm around me, adding, "Poor man was so scared he might lose her. And when he came back inside, called by the midwife, he was so relieved that Mama hadn't died, he let her name you."

"Snow in Summer," I said.

She nodded. "Snow in Summer. Like the white flowers that cover the front yard." She patted the divan, with its floral poplin covering. "Like this."

Then she gave me a hug. "Your daddy laughed and said, 'We gonna call her all that? *Snow in Summer?* Don't you

• • • • • • • •

think she's too tiny for such a big name?' 'We gonna call her Summer,' your mama told him. 'It's warm and pretty, just as warm and pretty as she is.' "

"I am," I said. "Warm."

"And *pretty*," Cousin Nancy said, drawing me closer. "Just like your mama."

That made me smile, of course. Everyone needs someone to tell them they look pretty. Especially at nine.

"You're pretty, too," I said to her, touching her cheek. Anyways, she was to me.

She smiled back. "And then your mama told your papa: 'Don't you worry, Lemuel . . .' " That was Papa's full name and Mama always said it that way though everyone else called him Lem. " 'She'll grow into the rest.' "

And so I was known as Summer, as long as Mama was alive. As long as Papa could remember I was alive after she died.

· · · · · · · ·

·2·

DO-LESS

fter she died.

After Mama died and spring came again, and then summer, Papa became do-less. He hadn't the energies to tend our gardens and they all began to run to weed and seed, the greens bolting like horses let out of an open stable door.

He hardly ate anything that wasn't put in front of him, and even then he seemed to forget it, his spoon left sitting in the porridge or his fork sticking up in the greens.

· · · · · · · ·

Cousin Nancy tackled the house garden early morning before opening the post office and again mid-morning when she closed the post office to take a mighty long lunch. And when I'd get back from school, I helped best I could. But I was only seven, and then eight and now nine, and though I was strong enough and willing, there was just so much I could do, that and no more.

Papa had never let anyone work in his gardens before. He was, everyone said, the spit of the old man, meaning Scottish grandpap. In fact, he was the only Morton cousin around who didn't go off hunting. They'd be out for hours, days even, coming home with deer and rabbits and partridge and coon, so many they had to be hauled back on sledges. No one went hungry in those days. The woods was a larder.

But Papa was the one Morton who didn't go out hunting. He had Grandpap's green fingers and everything he planted grew so tall it was like one of those stories people told at night around the fireplace when the kinfolk got together.

So Papa got to farm all that good bottomland, because no other Morton really wanted it. And if anyone complained, they did it to themselves, because he was generous to kin and anyway he did all the work. In between plowing

· · · · · · · ·

and fertilizing and planting the rows, he sang to the plants. He said it was the singing that made the green grow.

But after Mama died, his green fingers seemed to shrivel up, too, as if she'd been the one with green magic and not him. All to once, he gave over the gardens to Cousin Nancy and me. In fact, he didn't seem to notice we were there at all, on our hands and knees, trying to corral the runaways, weeding between the drooping plants. It was a drier-than-usual summer, the sun beating down on us without mercy.

While Cousin Nancy weeded and hoed, I was in charge of bringing water from the garden pump, a job that two summers earlier I'd begged Papa to let me try. Now I did all the pumping without Papa's permission or help. I hauled it in a tin bucket to wherever Cousin Nancy needed it, and my shins were black and blue for the whole of that summer where the full bucket banged against them.

My hands developed blisters that grew round, sore, and gray, then popped. Cousin Nancy put a lemon bee balm poultice on my hands at night and I slept with them wrapped up in white handkerchiefs soaked in the stuff until the blisters hardened into little calluses.

Often I simply dumped the last of the water from the tin bucket on myself to cool my fevered head. But neither the plants nor I were prospering in the heat.

. . . .

"I know you're tired and hot, Summer," Cousin Nancy said, shaking her head at me as I stood with the water dripping down. "But without this garden, you and your papa will have little enough to eat and nothing put up for winter." Then she gave me a hug and called me her big girl, her young heroine. "Like Molly Whuppie," she said, "who saved her sister and herself from the wicked giant."

So between telling me the truth of my family history and telling me fairy tales, between praising me and cozening me, Cousin Nancy and I worked the house garden. And with just the two of us we about managed. But neither of us was prepared to work on the big market garden out back. And without that garden, Papa and I would have nothing to sell down in Addison or Webster, nothing to go to Cogar's Grocery or to the big hotel on Main Street, where people came to take the waters of the salt sulfur springs.

Cousin Nancy pushed Papa as much as she could, as much as she dared, but he hardly listened. Or he was listening to some voice other than hers.

The few vegetables she coaxed from the big plot were nowhere near as good as Papa's. No one's were. He'd a genius for growing. Or he did once. But like his mind, like his heart, that genius was gone, buried in the grave with Mama.

· · · · · · · ·

By the fall, our neighbors were wondering instead if he'd gone sick, pining for Mama. "He'll be dead by winter," they said.

By the next year, they were worried silly about him. "He can't go on like this," they said.

By the time I was nine, they were calling him names. "Maybe he's turned queer in the head," said someone down at Cogar's. That diagnosis quickly made its way all around the town.

The kids in school, of course, took their ideas from their parents' gossip. Travis Cogar, who was in my class and sweet on me, told the third-grade boys that his mama said that Papa had been howling at the moon. And later that day I found a crudely drawn picture of Papa sitting on his haunches, head thrown back, clearly baying like a hound. Underneath it said, *Lemyule, the niht houler.* I knew Travis had written it since he'd been sending me badly spelled love notes since the start of second grade. Spelling—like the definition of words—had always been my best subject and I was very particular about it. I crumpled the picture in my hand and dropped it in Travis's lap where it belonged.

"Traitor!" I said. "Polecat!" I spoke the last loud enough for all the kids to hear. I actually sort of like the little critters though they stink something fierce if you bother them, raising that tail and stamping their little feet and throwing that smell over everything good. Just like Travis had just done.

At recess someone else called him a polecat, too, and pretty soon all the kids in school—all forty-seven of us in grades one through eight—held their noses when he went by, though I didn't encourage it.

He never sent me notes again.

I told Cousin Nancy what was being said in school, and she acknowledged it was being said elsewhere as well.

"Rumor," she told me dismissingly, "runs faster than truth. But truth gets there in the end."

However, rumor had run right up and deposited its stinking message on my desk. Truth didn't seem to be anywhere around.

·3·

DANCES AND SONGS

ot only did Papa sing to the plants. Once upon a time he sang to me, too.

"So you can grow like a little weed," he'd say.

And Mama would answer just as quick as quick, "Not a weed but a flower."

"Not a flower but a pumpkin."

"A daisy."

· · · · · · · ·

17

"Cabbage."

"Bloodroot."

"Runner bean."

"Violet."

"Ramps."

"Rose," I'd finally interject into my parents' long list.

Nobody ever won these arguments since we all fell about laughing the minute I said *rose,* though I never knew why. Then Papa would pick up his banjo again and play us some of the old tunes. And once in a while, he'd pick out a new tune he'd written just for Mama and me. One I specially recall had lines that went:

> *"My two ladies are just like roses,*
> *Pink from their heads to their pretty little toeses.*
> *All day, all night, everyone supposes*
> *That they are full of thorns."*

That's what I remember most about the old days, when we were three. Stories, jokes, music, and laughter.

Then of a sudden, it was all, all gone.

Papa and Mama had known each other from high school and got engaged the same time as Nancy Clarke got herself

· · · · · · · ·

hitched to Papa's favorite cousin, Jack Morton, who later was one of the first men killed on a beach somewhere in France right before I turned seven.

Cousin Nancy told me, "You were not expected but hoped for."

I recalled the wildflowers that Mama had loved, their names and what they were useful for. Her favorites had been bloodroot and trillium and wild violets.

Papa had loved wildflowers because of her. But he tended garden flowers and vegetables so they could be sold down at the Addison town market or carted off to Webster or even Clarksburg and Morgantown for the city folk who'd no bottomland of their own.

Twice a week, he'd pack the old truck full of vegetables and drive through the night to get to those far places in time for the farmer's market, coming home that evening with not a thing left to sell, dollars stuffed in the pockets of his overalls. And even though on market days he'd come home so tired he needed toothpicks to keep his eyes open—or so he said—he'd take out his banjo and sing to us while Mama and I danced all around the living room. *Heel and toe and away we'd go!* She and I held hands and swung till my feet left the ground. I remember that, too.

· · · · · · · ·

I recalled some of Mama's songs, too, like "All the Pretty Little Horses." Especially the part where Mama sang: *"Blacks and bays, dapples and grays . . . all the pretty little horses."*

Oh, and, *"Papa's gonna buy you a diamond ring."*

Of course *that* never happened. He didn't buy *me* a diamond ring or anything else. He was now, Cousin Nancy said, a "man of constant sorrow" like the old song goes.

Back then, it was Cousin Nancy who'd bought me the navy blue dress with the white bib and the navy blue coat with the matching hat that I wore as I trudged up to the grave site alongside Papa. That and the big boots. She got them all at a church tent sale down in Webster. Because I hadn't any decent enough clothing to wear to Mama's burying, all the rest being pinafores and overalls and sack dresses in bright flowered prints that Mama had made on her old Singer sewing machine with the foot treadle.

I reminded her of that dress, those boots.

"Couldn't have you going up to the graveside with your fanny hanging out of those old overalls," Cousin Nancy said, and I laughed, suddenly recalling those overalls. My, how I'd loved them. They were fourth or fifth hand by the time I got them and Mama had sewn little pink

. . . .

flowers all up and down the legs. She used to decorate all my clothes with hand-sewn embroidered flowers.

I pranced around the post office room pretending that my bottom was stuck out till Cousin Nancy was laughing along with me. We laughed a lot together. It was better than crying. We'd already done a whole lot of that.

Each year that I grew bigger and taller, Cousin Nancy got clothes for me, though always secondhand. Some were hand-downs from children of the town, others from the church charity shops. As she said of herself, "I was never much for sewing, not like your mama. But I can always find a bargain."

And, after all, the country was deep into the Depression. West Virginia had never been a rich man's place anyway. We all knew how to make do.

Of course, the hat and coat that I wore in the burial picture and the boots have long since been passed along to some other poor child in need. Not to any of the Morton cousins. They'd have thought that bad luck. But to someone way off in Cooleyville or Onego or Erbacon, or even farther, maybe all the way to Clarksburg.

Papa was so deep in his grief, he probably *would* have let me walk in my raggedy overalls behind the coffin. Or

· · · · · · · ·

21

left me at home all alone to cry myself to sleep. And even though Cousin Nancy was still in mourning for her Jack, she didn't throw herself into that grief the way Papa did.

"A woman hasn't time for such," she told me when I asked. "Life goes on."

"Mama's didn't," I whispered, "nor Cousin Jack's."

We both sat close for a quick cuddle and cry, the photo album put aside for later. Then we made a batter cake, which helped us both feel a lot better. I took a slice home for Papa, but he never ate a bite.

• 4 •

COUSIN NANCY REMEMBERS

 emuel Morton was the hand-somest boy in our class in Addison even in elementary school. And the sweetest. When we all went up to Webster for high school, that sweetness only grew.

Of course, all the Morton boys were handsome in a way, but none of the rest of them could be called sweet. Not even my Jack. They were hunters and most of them

· · · · · · · ·

were hard boys and harder men. They had to be, out in the mountains all day and half the night. They were never lost, though. Or as Jack used to joke about that, "Nope, never been lost, but I've been bothered for a day or two at a time."

But Lem had plant dreams in his fingertips. And my, how those things grew. Sunflowers big as trees, melons you could play basketball with, pole beans that sagged heavy on their sticks. He sang to his plants, too, which seemed to make them grow in wild profusion: cressy greens and dandelions for both salad and wine, corn and squash, dock and cabbage, and more kinds of beans than you could shake a stick at.

I think most all the other girls in our class thought Lem was too soft. He didn't hunt, he loved plants, and he read those books about aliens, starships, and faraway worlds that the general store sold, there not being a library in town. No one knew why he read such things, but I always figured it was because he wanted to find an explanation for the magic in his fingers. His wife, Ada Mae, said it was because he wanted to know why he was different, almost alien, from all the other boys in town. However, I loved him from the time we were six-year-olds at school.

Oh, I was plenty happy with my Jack. He'd the wryest sense of humor and was a loving man. I loved Lem in a

· · · · · · · ·

24

different way. We four—Jack and Lem and Ada Mae and me—spent many hours singing and laughing and playing jokes on one another in front of their fireplace, while baby Summer lay sleeping in her cradle.

I didn't change my mind about Lem Morton even when he went crazy from grief. I'd never expected anything to come of my love for Lem, though everyone else in town and certainly all his kin considered that we two—widow and widower—would soon be married. Instead I gave my love over to Summer, when she needed it most. I would have given my everlasting soul for the two of them.

And I guess I almost did.

· · · · · · ·

·5·

BESOT

wo years later, when I was eleven, Papa had begun tending his garden again. His green fingers still held their magic, but he no longer sang to his plants.

He no longer sang to me.

The only place he sang anymore was up at the old abandoned Morton church, sitting by Mama's grave. He'd go there every evening, when Cousin Nancy and I began to wash the dinner dishes. Pushing his chair back from the table, he'd say with nary a smile, "Another fine dinner, Nan," grab his banjo, and be gone.

I'd settle in to doing my homework, and Cousin Nancy would work a quilt on the dining room table till he returned. He never actually asked her to stay with me, but he never actually asked her not to, either. We were quiet company together. And Papa knew she'd keep me safe.

Now even with all his way with growing things, Papa never brought flowers up to Mama's grave. That was Cousin Nancy's business. And mine. She'd cut flowers from Papa's garden but let me gather wildflowers like pokeweed and yellow foxglove and the pretty blue-rayed asters that grew along the borders of the fields. And we'd walk up every week in the growing season to put the flowers on Mama's grave of a Sunday after church. But Cousin Nancy wouldn't let me pick any of the fuzzy snow whites that grew all about the edges of the grave-yard. "That's snakeroot," she warned me. "It brings on milk fever."

"I'm too old to get milk fever," I told her.

"That'll only make it worse," she said. Her voice was firm and I learned, once Cousin Nancy put her foot down, it stayed flat on the floor and she could not be budged.

· · · · · · · ·

Papa always cleared the flowers we left on Mama's grave the very next evening. He said he couldn't stand to see them curling up, growing black at the tips and dying so quickly, cut off from the sod.

Cousin Nancy kept telling him that if he'd give her permission, she'd plant something on Mama's grave for him. "So there'd be *something* growing there."

But Papa gave her a black look whenever she proposed it, though otherwise he was still a sweet-natured man. "If *she* can't be growing beside me," he said, meaning Mama, "then I want that grave to be stark."

And stark it was. Even grass didn't grow on it. It looked like a scar on the churchyard's green mantle, just as Mama's death was a scar on Papa's heart.

Cousin Nancy didn't give up, though—not for the longest time. I loved her even more for that. "A climbing rose might be nice," she offered once, "or a bunch of early snowdrops. Little purple crocuses come fall?"

Another black look from Papa. A shrug. A grunt instead of a kind word in return. It made me wonder about True Love.

Oh, we knew where he was going when he went out after dinner, and we let him get on with it. There was no stopping him anyway, not even the time I had influenza bad and Cousin Nancy had to bathe me in lukewarm water

. . . .

28

to get my fever down. He had his banjo and his sorrow, and he was away.

There were still sweet times with him out in the garden, where he showed me how to coax snowdrops out by pulling away the heavy pack of snow from their roots. And days when he taught me how to pick the green cabbage caterpillars and aphids and caterpillar eggs off the leaves and squash them. We even made up a squashing song with a chorus of "Squish, squash, ugh! Go away, bug!" that had me howling with laughter and Papa smiling a little.

And there were times he would look at me and sigh. "You do so look like your mama, Summer." And then he would touch the top of my head as gentle as could be, as if he feared I might break at his touch.

But mostly he was distant.

Not mean.

Not cold.

Just not there.

About that time, I began starting fights with Cousin Nancy, being sassy to her, not heeding a thing she said. And when she told me to "Mind your manners, missy," I'd snap back, "You don't tell him to!" Meaning Papa.

"He's a grown man and a sorrowing man," she said.

· · · · · · · ·

"Well, I'm still sorrowing, too," I shouted at her, though I wasn't. I ran into my room and slammed the door. She didn't come in for long minutes and when she did, she sat down beside me on my bed and said, "He'll come through it, Summer. I promise he will. And so will you."

But I thought I had nowhere to come *to*. Papa was *that* far away.

Only one day Papa came down from the mountain with a woman none of us had ever met and only I'd clapped eyes on her before. He was set on marrying her, even given her his grandmother's diamond ring, the one that was too big and gaudy for Mama, though she'd kept it in her jewelry box, letting me play with it every now and then.

"Too soon. Too soon," Cousin Nancy said, though it wasn't all that soon, not really. It'd been almost four years since Mama's death, since we'd walked up to the mountain graveyard and set her down. Everyone else in town thought it was well beyond time.

I know that everyone, me included, had been expecting Papa to marry Cousin Nancy after he left off grieving. I think Cousin Nancy expected it, too. Though we hadn't known he'd left it off till he came down the mountainside with that woman.

· · · · · · · ·

"Your poor mama hardly stiff in her grave, and that . . ." Cousin Nancy hesitated. "That *witch*." I think she had a different word in mind, though back when she said it, I wouldn't have known what the other word was anyway. Or would've taken it instead for a hound dog's mama. "That *witch* has him besot."

It was a long time before I understood the true meaning of that word. *Besot* means "muddled." "Fuddled." "Bewitched." "Charmed." A fairy-tale word for a terrible condition, one that about killed him and me, too.

While I hardly remembered Mama and the baby or the burial excepting as it is in the photograph, I surely recall how the rest all fell out and will till my dying day. It happened this way.

As usual Papa went to the graveyard after dinner. He'd been at it for more than three years and didn't look like he was ever going to change.

And as usual, I was not allowed to go along. He said he liked the lonely walk up the mountain. His mood matched the owls' and other night birds' mournful calling. "Like a long, sad song," he said.

Cousin Nancy was brushing my hair a hundred strokes, till it seemed my hair was a-crackle with little lightning

. . . .

bugs. Then she yanked at my hair a bit too hard. I pulled away, my upset with Papa turning into an upset with her.

"Ow, you're pulling. You're a cruel old . . ."

"Didn't mean to, honey. But you gotta sit still and not wiggle." She gathered up a hank of my hair again.

I was in such a fidget that day. "If Papa can come and go as he pleases, why can't I?"

"Because you're not quite eleven years old, that's why." She sighed. "And your papa isn't doing this to spite you, child, it's just that he's partial to the way those graves look in the fading light."

I understood what she meant, how the dark shadows humped up, then slowly filled in all the little potholes and gullies. Dusk fit Papa's mood. He was in no mind to share it with anyone else. And he'd gotten used to it. He didn't care what anyone else thought of his grief, though surely he knew the town folk and his Morton kin thought he should move on.

"There's nowhere to move on *to*," is what he said.

"He should move on to you," I'd told Cousin Nancy more than once, but she always shushed me, saying, "Some folk never move on from a grief like that." And I didn't know when she said it if she was talking about Papa or herself.

The women at church where I went with Cousin Nancy whispered about Papa's *excess*. One even went so

· · · · · · · ·

far as to say, "He's wallowing in his grief like a pig in a mud hole."

Cousin Nancy shushed her just as readily as she'd shushed me. "You can't put a counter on True Love," she told them, "even after death. The heart wants what it wants, even when it can't have it."

True Love, I thought. Just like in the stories. Papa's love for Mama was for all eternity. And then, uncomfortably, I thought: *If this is real life, it's much harder than anything I've ever read about.*

Winter had turned to spring, and the wildflowers marched across the mountains like an army of invaders. Once again Cousin Nancy tried to reason with Papa.

I had just woken up in my little bedroom off the kitchen and I could hear Papa stirring in the living room, rousing up from the overstuffed living room chair where he'd collapsed in sorrow after coming down from the mountain, a thing that had become a usual sleeping place for him.

Cousin Nancy was already in the house making us breakfast, which she did every morning excepting Sundays, when she collected me to go straight off to church. She wasn't a Baptist like Papa and me but a Catholic and she worshipped in the tiny church down behind Main Street with only a handful of other folk. When Mama was alive,

· · · · · · · ·

I'd never have set foot in Cousin Nancy's church. Baptists just didn't do that then. But by that time I was almost a member of the Roman religion.

Truth to tell, I loved the beautiful window at Cousin Nancy's church with the pretty painting of Jesus pictured on the glass. He held his heart in his hand. It reminded me a bit of Papa and how he sometimes looked at me with a gaze that held eternity. And the simple wooden crucifix and the statue of Mary roughly carved out of wood, and the hand-stitched altar furnishings that the Ladies Union had sewn, in white and blue for everyday masses, but in deep purple for the holy days.

This morning, Cousin Nancy leaned in over Papa with a vase full of lupine as blue as church glass. Setting it in the middle of the end table, she said as casually as she could, "I can make the grave look real pretty, Lem. Ada Mae would have liked that." It was the first time in months Cousin Nancy had asked. Maybe the spring had made her bold. Maybe it had given her hope.

I stood at the door of my bedroom and held my breath, waiting to see if this time Papa would change his mind.

He didn't shrug or throw a black look in her direction. Instead he made a growling noise low in his throat, like a wounded animal. Then he shook himself all over. "I honor your intentions, Nan," he said at last, "but nothing could be

. . . .

worse, knowing that everything will rise up in the spring but her." He never said Mama's name anymore, just *she* and *her* and *my wife,* as if naming her might somehow put a curse on her. Then he stood and walked out the door, turning for a moment to say, "I won't hear a word more about it." Then off he went to work in the gardens, to plow all his grief and longing into the soil.

I shook my head and watched him go, then got myself ready for school, brushing my own hair and braiding it up the best I could. I didn't want to hear a word more about it, either. If there was to be a war between the two people I loved most in this world, I wouldn't take sides.

That evening Cousin Nancy set the vase with the lupines plumb in the middle of the dinner table, right next to the roast chicken, without saying a word. But she didn't have to. He knew what she meant. And *he'd* meant what he'd said.

He didn't bother sitting down at the table. Just grabbed up a chicken leg in one hand, his banjo in the other, kicked open the screen door, and went out. He was going up the mountain as usual to sit on Mama's grave, his back against the simple stone cross. We knew where he was going. He'd told us so before. His face would be turned toward the other graves, their stones patchworked with lichen over their long inscriptions. Papa never wanted more than

· · · · · · · ·

Mama's name and dates on her stone. No *Rest with Jesus,* or *Beloved Wife and Mother,* or any such. Just *Ada Mae Morton 1920–1944.*

And there he'd stay, on her mound, playing his banjo and singing the old tunes, probably the ones she'd loved best. "Pretty Polly," and "Tom Dula," and of course "Shady Grove." But he wouldn't play for me anymore. Just played there, on the grave. Try explaining that to an almost eleven-year-old.

Cousin Nancy tried, of course. She never stopped trying.

But that evening, something got into me. Something devilish maybe. Or someone else watching over me. I jumped up, too, and ran out after Papa, leaving Cousin Nancy alone in the house with the dinner uneaten and that vase of blue flowers sitting accusingly on the table.

The sun was about an hour from setting down behind Elk Mountain as I traipsed after Papa to the grave site. I didn't need to hurry. I knew where he was going. Besides, he was a tall man with a long stride. I couldn't have caught up to him had I tried.

I didn't want to chance him sending me home with another one of his black looks. So I stayed back out of sight and walked as quiet as I could. Night birds were singing around me, and there was a kind of buzzing in the air.

. . . .

Every now and again I glimpsed Papa a long way ahead of me. He never looked back to see me trailing him. It was enough that I'd soon be with him at Mama's grave.

When I got to the church, I made my way around to the back where the churchyard sat, but quietly. I could hear the thread of music coming from his banjo. He was in the middle of "Shady Grove."

I sneaked over to a place by one of the biggest gravestones and hunched down behind it, hidden in the shadows. Now that I was here, I'd suddenly gotten cold feet about showing myself to him, about sitting down at his side while he played on Mama's grave. What could I say to him? Would he be as mad at me as he was at Cousin Nancy? I sank down onto the ground, it barely warm from the afternoon sun, and watched.

His eyes were tight shut, and he sang along with the banjo: "Shady grove, my true love, I'm bound to go away." His voice was low and confiding.

Turned out, I wasn't the only watcher that evening. I heard a small sound and saw a woman standing on the other side of the churchyard, the mountain side, right next to a tall gravestone. Tall and slender, almost bony, she was silent as a *haint,* a ghost. The skin stretched tight over her

· · · · · · ·

37

cheekbones—like parchment. But though she was slim, the woman wasn't anywhere near gaunt as some of the women around here who've been eking out a hardscrabble life for years. This woman was thin but beautifully so, her hair shagged, not in the braids or the rolls other women hereabouts wore. Her mouth had been reddened with a slash of red lipstick that looked near black in the shadows thrown by the setting sun. Later, I'd see that she had one blue eye and one green. Not a word did she say to make herself known, she just stood there gazing deeply and longingly at Papa.

At last, she came around the gravestone and sat down on a black slab gravestone close by him, still staring as if she could eat him up. I knew then she wasn't a haint but a real live person because black grave slabs keep in the heat of the sun. Everybody knows that. And a haint wouldn't be able to stand the heat.

Tucking her dark skirt up under her knees, she crossed her ankles. They were pretty ankles, covered in sheer stockings. None of the women in Webster County that I knew around here had such finery. They couldn't afford it. They simply drew lines on the backs of their legs to make it look like stocking seams. Mama got to wear sheer stockings only on the day of her wedding.

· · · · · · · ·

The woman never once showed by a single glance that she saw me watching her, but there was an unnatural awareness about her. It took me years to figure out that she'd known I was there even before I'd ever seen her. But at the moment, I was alert to her, all the while thinking myself well hidden.

She cleared her throat and Papa looked up. She crooked her pointer finger at him, the nail as reddened as her lips.

Did Papa fall in love that instant? I was never to know for real. But that woman radiated a power, or so Cousin Nancy would say later. The kind of magic that wraps a man around her finger and drives him to the brink of madness. I don't know if it was True Love, but Papa was plumb crazy from that moment on.

He stopped singing and was struck dumb. Simple as that. It was as if he'd drunk a whole jug of Hank Gregory's moonshine down in one long swallow. Fuddled. That's what he was.

"Stupefied," Cousin Nancy said when she saw him. "With the emphasis on the *stupe*."

The woman smiled at him, those red-black lips opening like a snake's. She showed no teeth. And then, without speaking, she disappeared.

Disappeared.

. . . .

I gawped at the slab where she'd been sitting. I hadn't even seen her stand up. Yes, maybe I'd blinked once. Even twice. But no true human could have moved *that* fast. One moment there, then gone.

Once again I thought: a haint! But why a ghost who looked like that should have been walking about the Elk Mountain churchyard, I'd no idea. She wasn't any Morton I'd ever known.

Papa was too fuddled to see me, and he tried to start playing his banjo again. But one of the strings had broken in two, and neither of us had even heard it twang. So he stood, shouldered the instrument, and, as if walking in a dream, started back down the mountain. But after three steps, he stumbled, going down heavily onto his knees.

Only then did I rush forward to put my arms around him, hauling him back up to his feet and crying out, "Papa! Papa!"

He hardly noticed it was me. Didn't say my name or ask why I was up there in the first place. I pulled his free hand around my shoulder and he left it there. And supporting him as best I could, we managed one difficult step at a time to get down the mountain and home.

Cousin Nancy had cleared away the uneaten dinner and was sitting on the divan, her fingers twined together, when we came in. She jumped up, then gathered Papa in her arms.

. . . .

"Take the banjo, child," she told me, "and set it against the wall."

I did as she said, putting it right where Papa always kept it, next to his big chair, while Cousin Nancy hustled him off to his bed. He was like a dead man walking. So she just plunked him down, still in his clothes and boots.

When she came back into the living room, she didn't ask me what had happened up there on the mountain. I think she knew I'd tell it in my own time. All she said was, "I'll be by in the morning. If he's no better, send for the doctor."

But I knew he was just enchanted, and by then, I was the real sick one. My throat was on fire, whether from the cold air or the fear or the strangeness of the evening, I didn't know. But it hurt so bad I'd begun to cry.

"Can't hardly talk," I told Cousin Nancy, pointing to my throat. So she had me gargle with honey and vinegar and put me right to bed without even nagging me about my homework.

"I swear," Cousin Nancy said, more to herself than to me, "it's as if this family is as broken as that banjo string." And shaking her head, she went out to the living room to read until she thought that Papa and I had both fallen asleep, before she was willing to go off home.

I didn't think she was happy about leaving even then, but she wasn't worried that Papa was crazy enough to do

· · · · · · · ·

something wicked. Besides, it wasn't really her house and it wasn't really her place to be there, and if she'd stayed overnight, tongues would surely wag in town about it. That's how it is in a small place like Addison. But still—as she told me years later—she didn't sleep a wink that night, just paced up and down until the morning light.

Papa didn't actually sleep a wink, either. I heard him tossing and turning all night. And the one time I got up to check on him, he was back in the living room, sitting gazing into the hearth. He wasn't singing or reading his books, just staring at the cold coals and mumbling, his fingers picking at an invisible banjo because the real one was still against the wall beside the chair.

He never took up the banjo again till years later.

When I woke, starving for my breakfast, my sore throat was all gone. I was well again, or well enough, but Papa wasn't. He was still staring into the coals and playing music on something he didn't have in his hands.

The kids at school might have called him a *jake*, but I knew better.

Just like in the old stories, he was caught in a woman's wiles. He was well and truly besot.

· · · · · · · ·

·6·

UP AND DOWN THE MOUNTAIN

fter he saw the woman that first time, and sat up all night staring into the coals, Papa was up the mountain a lot longer each night. Cousin Nancy had to stay with me later and later. She didn't complain about that because there was a spring in his step that had been missing for a while, missing ever since Mama had died.

I thought about how the strange woman had crooked her finger at Papa. Though I wanted to tell Cousin Nancy about

· · · · · · · · ·

it, and even tried once or twice, I couldn't seem to form the words. It was as if I, too, had been bewitched somehow.

As for Cousin Nancy—she didn't ask.

It was a huge gap between us. Like the place between mountains. Our first gap, but not our last.

Cousin Nancy's friends said that time had done its worst on Papa, but he was through now to the other side.

Through to the other side. They also said that about someone who's died. But maybe they weren't far wrong. He was on to another side. Only it wasn't the one they thought it was, nor me, either.

Papa began working the garden with renewed vigor. He got the market garden hoed and rowed and planted, seeded and weeded. He simply raced across the acres.

Cousin Nancy smiled to see him work that way and said to me out of his hearing, "I told you he'd come to his senses, Summer."

I smiled back and wanted it to be true. I loved Papa. I'd *missed* Papa. But he seemed too frantic to me. He barely ate, he hardly slept, and still he raced around. It seemed to me there was something almost unnatural about Papa's attention to his plants.

Still, when Miss Caroline and Miss Amelia, friends from Cousin Nancy's church, sat in her parlor one Sunday

· · · · · · · ·

after Mass, they were all amazed at Papa's renewed energy. We ate the cookies I'd helped Cousin Nancy make the day before. I got to pour the tea, my favorite part, tipping the pot just right till the hot dark umber liquid came shooting out the spout.

Miss Caroline said, "That Lemuel, he *sure* can work."

Holding her cup out for me to fill, Miss Amelia added, "He sure *can. Dancing* down the rows!" She said it all admiring.

After four years of sorrow, I'd become used to Papa's silent brooding. I thought I'd finally come to understand it. Was I the only one to worry about him being so unnatural?

Cousin Nancy passed the cookies. "God's mysterious ways," she said.

So I put my worries out of mind.

The seeds sprouted well before their catalog time. Perfect green thrusts in every row. And what did it matter that I hadn't recognized the newer things he planted or that they spread so fast, they seemed like invading armies? Papa was back with us and that was all that mattered.

God's mysterious ways indeed.

No one—not even Cousin Nancy or me—knew what was truly happening until a month later, with the garden all abloom with dark green shoots, and Papa stayed away from home till the next morning.

· · · · · · · ·

Cousin Nancy had slept all night in the chair in our living room, waiting for him to come home so she could go to her own house and bed. I found her there when I rose in the morning and went out to the privy first thing before sunrise.

Papa returned when Cousin Nancy was making me toast with jam, and with him was the woman, the haint who'd disappeared before my very eyes that night. In broad daylight she looked more like a model in one of Cousin Nancy's *Life* magazines. Papa walked with her down from the mountain and all the way—so it was said by one of the Morton cousins who'd been out jacking a deer and saw them—she sashayed like she belonged by his side.

And that's when Cousin Nancy and everyone in town found out the thing I already knew—Papa was besot.

He'd gone up the mountain that May night a widower and come down a tied man. Seems he'd given the woman with the red slash of a mouth Great-Grammy's ring to bind her to him. And bound she seemed to be, holding on to his arm as if she owned it and him along with it. Owned his body—and maybe something more.

Though who was the most bound, it was hard to say.

When they came to our little house, they unaccountably stood outside the door. Cousin Nancy and I could hear Papa laughing, the kind of deep belly laugh we hadn't

. . . .

heard since Mama and the baby died. And then another laugh, a softer, secret sound, full of something whispery.

Cousin Nancy was busy making our breakfast, so she said, "Summer, get the door." There was something tense in her voice, something angry, too.

I threw the door wide and there was Papa and the woman, and they were touching each other in a way that made Cousin Nancy sniff. Not the sniff that the ladies of our church would later give, but a kind of sad little sniff, full of lost opportunities and old times gone by. I noticed it right off but didn't understand it enough to turn and question her. Nor, I think, would she have told me then. But after the sniff, she set down the jam knife carefully on the plate, set her shoulders back, and nodded at Papa but not the woman as she went through the front door, with nary a word. Her back was straight as the haint woman's seams. As straight as a soldier's off to war.

Soon as Cousin Nancy had left, Papa said to me, "Aren't you gonna invite this lady in?" which seemed a strange thing to say, seeing it was Papa's own house.

The woman smiled, though it never seemed to light her eyes, and she crooked her finger at me.

"Of course, Papa, if that's what you want," I said, and stood out of the way as they both came in.

· · · · · · · ·

"This," Papa said, nodding at me and neglecting to say the woman's own name—if indeed he knew it then—"this is my daughter, Snow in Summer."

The woman looked straight at me as though she could see down into my heart and found me wanting. I gave a little shiver for it felt as if a cold wind had blown right through me.

"That's too big a name for such a little girl," she said to me. "I'm going to call you Snow." Her voice was careful and tight as if speaking with a child was a new skill she was trying to learn.

I opened my mouth to protest that I was called *Summer*, but no sound came out. So, I looked over at Papa, expecting him to explain. But he was rapt, charmed by her.

I wanted to leave the house and follow Cousin Nancy, who must have been at her own house already, but my feet felt rooted to the floor. That was it—rooted. Tied in a different way than Papa, but tied nonetheless.

The woman sat down prettily and carefully on one of the nearest chairs, the old walnut rocker that had rocked me to sleep when I was a baby and my daddy when he was a little boy before me. She reached out an elegant hand to me. I found I had a new strength, a kind of giddiness, and almost skipped over to where she sat. Then that hand,

· · · · · · · ·

strong as a vise, curled around my upper arm and she drew me—not entirely unwilling then—up onto her lap.

"We're going to be such good friends, Snow," she said to me in her cool voice. "I've so much to teach you." Her hands were not at all like Cousin Nancy's, which were always soft and warm. This new woman's hands were cold as ice cut from a winter pond, and as hard.

Only then did I try to pull away, but of course she was too strong for me and I had to stay, uncomfortably perched on her lap like a cat on a patch of ice.

She whispered in my ear, the voice sweet as honey. Sweeter. "You can call me Mama."

"Ma . . ."

"Mama," she repeated.

"Ma . . ."

I tried to say it, the word pooling in my mouth like sour sick-up. But I couldn't.

Not then.

Not ever.

Stepmama was the closest I could manage.

Close enough.

STEPMAMA REMEMBERS

 only loved one man in my life. He taught me everything I know about the Craft. Brilliant, diamond hard, he looked like an eagle, all beak and bald head, with piercing golden eyes. He was everything I wanted, but he couldn't love me back. Oh, he admired me. He wanted me. He needed me. But he didn't love me.

So I had to kill him.

But I did it slowly and I didn't cause him any pain. After all, I'm not an evil woman.

Besides, he'd had my youth giving boost to his for seven years. And I gave it gladly. It was an exchange. He had seven years that he could not have had without me, and I learned the Craft. That is the way of it. The years freely given have power. The ones taken by force do not. They are just years.

Before the Master died, he shared more with me than his knowledge. He shared a secret.

"The Craft," he said, "has its limitations like any art. You cannot prosper from it directly. If you use the Craft for money, the art of it dies. And when the art dies, the power dies, too. So one must support the Craft in other ways."

"Other ways?" I opened my eyes wide. I was puzzled but as always eager to learn. He liked that in me, liked that I turned to him with questions. He thought he was in complete control, and so he told me without further prodding. But men are never the ones in control. Not if the woman is smart and steady, if she is able to disguise and swallow her disgust. Nothing makes a man angrier than seeing disgust or disdain in his woman's eyes.

So he told me. It was so simple but aren't all secrets simple, once revealed? Even in magic. Especially in magic.

· · · · · · · ·

Master had ways of teasing out secrets from the rich and powerful. Not using the Craft, of course, but magician's tricks, sleights of hand, distractions, refractions, inflections, reflections. Simple stuff. One of his rich followers was a railroad magnate in the process of setting up a system of train lines across the South. A spur was to go through the West Virginia mountains where poor people would be glad to sell their land for quick cash. So Master began buying up that property, a bit here and a bit there, for very small change and turning around to sell it on to the railroad tycoon at a huge profit.

In Webster County, though, there was a single holdout, a man whose ties to the land were stronger than his need for money. This my Master learned just days before I killed him, and he'd passed this information on to me. He went down into his final sleep smiling. I think he knew what I was doing and approved of it. After all, he was a very old man, his health shaky at best. Besides, he'd already gotten my seven years and would have needed another young person. In a way, killing him was my final test.

I shall miss Master every day of my life, but it is *my* life, not his, that brings me to this moment. He had no time to act on the final bit of information, and now I act in his stead. I located the Webster County man and the land. I

. . . .

could smell how strongly they were tied together. It would be a challenge to part them. But I've always enjoyed a challenge. And I have all the Craft at my fingertips to bind this poor farmer to me for richer and for poorer. In sickness and in health. For three years to bind the charm. Till death do us part. His death—not mine.

Still, I never planned to let him suffer overmuch. He was a handsome man, so I toyed with him for a while. Cat and mouse. Of course the cat always wins this battle.

And his daughter. That was a surprise. A perfect peach of a child. My first thought was to bring her into the Craft. I had plenty of time to win her trust. She was a long ways from becoming a woman, her moon courses years from their running. I promised myself I'd take her seven years. But I knew that even if she wouldn't give them to me willingly and I had to kill her along with her father, neither of them would die in pain.

After all, I'm not a wicked woman.

· · · · · · · ·

·8·

TIES THAT BIND

ach evening for a month while they planned their wedding, Papa walked Stepmama back up the mountain as if he was walking her home. As if she could have a home up there amongst the gravestones. He never wondered where she lived. That's how I knew he was thoroughly bewitched.

The wedding—such as it was—didn't come quick enough for some and came much too quick for others. It took place

· · · · · · · ·

at the Town Hall, that old pile of stones, an uncomfortable and uncomforting building, cold and echoing. Stepmama wouldn't step foot in either Papa's church or Cousin Nancy's. And even besot, Papa refused to get married at the old Morton church amongst the gravestones. It was the only time he argued with Stepmama that I can recall.

The town clerk administered the wedding vows, in a husky voice more used to registering voters than binding lovers. He smiled at them with false teeth that looked ready to fall out of his mouth and clattered as he spoke.

Papa's *I do* was swift and happy. Stepmama's response just quick. But it was over in seconds, and Papa bent to kiss the bride, who turned her cheek to him.

There was a table of sweets laid out in the hall, mostly brought in by Cousin Nancy and her friends. Stepmama had supplied the drinks: last season's apple cider, sharp and tangy, for the grown-ups, as well as iced sweet tea. She was minding that many of the town folks coming along to the wedding were teetotal. Of course there was milk for the children, though except for me and one or two of my school friends brought by their parents, there were few of those who attended.

Mr. Myerson of Myerson's Studio in Cowan was called in to take the official wedding picture. There was to be only one. "Why would we need more?" Stepmama told Papa.

. . . .

There was no dancing, no music. Stepmama said country songs hurt her ears. Everyone was sent home early.

It didn't matter. Papa looked happy. Ecstatic. And that was what counted.

We three walked back to the house together and I was sent immediately to my room. It was only five in the afternoon, but Stepmama said they would see me in the morning and closed my door behind her with a sharp, final click.

I didn't know exactly what newlyweds did besides live Happy Ever After. But clearly they did it without their children about. So I climbed up onto my bed, took out my fairy-tale book, and read a half dozen or more stories.

I must have fallen asleep at some point for I woke with a full moon shining through my window. Closing my book, I got into my nightclothes and slipped under the covers, where I was soon warm and cozy. This time when I fell asleep, I dreamed of Papa dancing along the garden rows, playing his banjo, and happy once more, singing loudly "False Knight on the Road."

The first thing they did after the wedding was their honeymoon trip to Ohio. I stayed at Cousin Nancy's the whole time. We waved as they drove off in Stepmama's little green car. She drove.

. . . .

"Not about to let Lemuel drive my baby," she said. "And not about to go away in his smelly old produce truck." She wrinkled her nose in a way that suggested she was joking, but I didn't think she was.

They were gone over a week, staying in a hotel that had a ballroom and everything. Not that Papa could dance.

They came home by way of Charleston, where she had all her things in storage. When they got back, her car was jammed with packets of odd seeds and leggy, long-leafed plants in gray pots that Papa and I helped bring into the house. All in all, about seven boxes of stuff. This didn't seem strange to me. After all, Papa was a gardener. Mama had loved flowers. Why shouldn't Stepmama have an interest in growing things, too? At eleven it seemed to me just another form of the fairy tale of True Love: that the green plants they both loved had brought them together.

Then Stepmama brought in the boxes of tall bottles in which dark-colored potions sloshed. She warned me sternly away from all of them.

"They could make you very sick, Snow," she cautioned, clinking a long red fingernail against the glass of the darkest bottle. Something almost seemed to stir in the depths, something with hands and feet and closed eyes. Something like a dead baby.

· · · · · · · ·

"Why do you have them, then?" I looked away from the horrible thing lurking in the bottle's darkness and then back again, for it drew my eyes in a way I couldn't explain.

"I do . . . experiments," she said, putting her hands on my shoulders and turning me around to face her.

I gazed into her differently colored eyes, the blue one on the right, the green one on the left. "We do experiments in school," I said.

She laughed, though it didn't sound as if she was particularly happy. "Probably not like these," she told me. "I try to understand things. Learn to control them." She said it in a whisper as if confiding in me.

"I understand," I said, though I didn't. Not then. I pulled away from her and turned back to the bottle, mesmerized by the dark, by what it promised, and put my hand to the bottle.

She pulled me back sharply. "Don't even *touch* the bottle, child," she said, voice suddenly coarsened, almost excited, "until I teach you the Way."

"The Way?"

"The bottles themselves can turn a person blue. Bring on the bloat. Scabies. Black tongue."

I wondered that they hadn't made *her* sick as well, or at least given her the agonies. But of course she had to know the Way, whatever that was.

. . . .

Suddenly I wondered why she'd brought the bottles into our house if they were that dangerous. Still, I heeded her warning and stayed away from the table on which the bottles sat though it took all my concentration to do so.

Next she opened a box that held a large mortar and pestle made of black stone, biggest one I ever saw. The one in our kitchen was tiny compared to it, and made of wood.

Big enough to crush whole bones, I thought, and shuddered, as if there was a tale there in the mortar, lurking behind its smooth surface, maybe a story about giants crushing humans and eating them alive. But I liked the smoothness of the mortar's side and how shiny the tip of the pestle was and how it fit exactly in Stepmama's hand. It was cool, sturdy, contained. *I can take a lesson from that,* I thought.

The rest of the boxes held Stepmama's clothes.

"You can help me shake them out, Snow," she said.

Summer, I thought. But Summer suddenly seemed very far away.

Stepmama also had a huge packet wrapped in black linen and tied securely with long pieces of twine. It was carted in, over the mountain. When the carters were paid and sent on their way, she unwrapped the thing and I saw it was a framed mirror on a large stand, a cross hanging down from

· · · · · · · ·

the bottom, and with words carved and painted in gold on the wood surround, words I couldn't read. Even though I loved books and had a whole shelf of them—the *Blue* and *Green* and *Orange Fairy* books, *The Wonderful Wizard of Oz*, *Just So Stories*, *The Secret Garden*, and a whole bunch of Raggedy Ann and Andy stories—I couldn't quite read what was carved in the mirror's wood frame. The sentences were in some foreign tongue. The two I remember best were *Acta est fabula* and *Corruptio optimi pessima*. I could almost make them out, but not really.

It was a very big mirror, almost as tall as me. I pressed my fingers to the letters when Stepmama's back was turned, as if I might puzzle out the meanings of the words that way. But once she caught me doing that and forbade me ever touch the mirror again.

"Will it bring bloat and scabies?" I asked.

She laughed. Her laugh was suddenly an unlikely fall of sound, like the tinkling of bells. "Why, child," she said, "are you tetched? You have the strangest notions." As if she'd forgotten the warning she'd given me before.

After that, Stepmama moved in all her perfumes and face paints, as well as a carved chair that had—so she told me—death and the maiden carved on one side. Then laughing, she added, "And taxes on the other."

. . . .

"What are taxes?" I asked.

Her fingers around my wrist drew me in and she whispered harshly, "A payment owed."

"I don't owe any payment," I told her. "I haven't any money. Papa doesn't allow it."

"There are many kinds of payment, Snow," she said, "and many ways to pay what is owed." She was smiling with that red slash of lips as she spoke. It was a big but not inviting smile.

I thought about the poor old women who sometimes bartered with Papa for his vegetables and seed corn, giving him in exchange a family portrait or an old gold watch belonging to some dead relative. About once a year he took such barter over to Clarksburg to sell, sharing what he got with the families who'd paid him in that way, giving them the greater part and taking out only what the vegetables and seed corn cost.

"When times are hard," Cousin Nancy had once told me when I asked where he was going and why, "it's not the time to drive a hard bargain. Not with your neighbors."

Remembering those barters, I nodded at Stepmama.

She took that as an understanding between us. But there was *nothing* between us. Not then. Not now. Though there has been a payment.

· · · · · · · ·

At first I wanted to be loved by Stepmama. Cousin Nancy had been forced out of my life, Stepmama insisting that she couldn't visit the way she had before.

"It isn't fit any longer that Cousin Nancy cooks your breakfast and brushes your hair, oversees your homework and puts you to bed," Stepmama explained. "That's my job as your new mama." She smiled, and though the smile wasn't particularly warm, I felt the warmth.

"And it isn't fitting that she's in and out of this house all times of the day and night like she did before, now that Lem is married." She said it in a way that made it sound like what Cousin Nancy had done for us had been, somehow, wrong.

And yet . . . and yet, I was sure she was being fair. Cousin Nancy hadn't been my *actual* mama. And there *was* a new woman in Papa's house now, a legitimate one, married forever after. Truly, the only one who suffered from this new rule was Cousin Nancy herself, for Papa and I were happily under Stepmama's spell.

So, at first I had what I really wanted. What a child wants is nothing more than unconditional love. I was too young to understand that Stepmama was not someone who gave that kind of love. Or any kind, as it turned out.

· · · · · · · ·

What she did was to barter or trade for the outward signs of love—a hug, a stroke along the arm, a kind word. Each of these things came with its own price.

But those first days seemed like heaven. She cozened me and coddled me and fed me on lies. And I believed them all.

Stepmama talked about being impressed with the mountains, the music, the people. She mentioned places by name. Songs as well. And she heaped high praise on Cousin Nancy once she was well and truly out of my life.

"A good woman," Stepmama said. "A caretaker."

"And Papa?" I asked, looking up into her face, seeing what I wanted to see, missing the rest. "You love Papa?"

Her eyes gave nothing away but her mouth smiled. She gave me a hug and said, "Of course, your papa most of all."

With that, I pushed closer to her than she was to me, my arms around her till I could feel her backbone stiffen. I thought it meant that she wanted me to hold her tighter. When I tightened as much as I could, she sighed.

"We have work to do, Snow," she'd say, twisting out of my embrace. Though what she really meant was that I had to go outside and rake or hoe or bring in salad greens while she did her nails. "Because you know the garden so much better than I do and I might do it harm," she told me.

· · · · · · · ·

And I never thought to ask why she had all those seeds and plants in her room then.

Or she meant that I was to scrub her underthings till my knuckles were bruised on the washboard. "Because your hands are small and my big old hands would likely damage my underclothes, in which I want to look lovely for your papa."

I truly wished at those moments that I could have called her "Mama," as she demanded. But though I thought my heart was willing, my mouth revolted, becoming as serpent-like as hers, refusing to speak the word aloud, no matter how often she insisted.

Still, I like to think that—in the early days, for a short while—we were both reasonably content. Why shouldn't we have been? We each had what we wanted, or at least what we thought we wanted. Me an attentive mother living in the house, she a biddable child who did all the work without complaint.

We had it then for a short while, but it was not to be what either of us would get for long.

The truth was: I was beguiled by Stepmama. That old word. It means "enchanted." "Deluded." "Cheated." "Charmed." Not besot like Papa, but close enough.

. . . .

·9·

COUSIN NANCY REMEMBERS

ould I have stopped Lem from marrying that woman? Sooner stop a runaway horse heading back to the barn. He had the bit tightly between his teeth. Besides, my own papa used to say that life is simpler when you plow *around* the stumps.

After all, Lem had married Ada Mae in the same feverish rush, and she turned into a sweet, lovely woman and an exceptional mother. Perhaps he'd just been lucky that time.

· · · · · · · ·

He was certainly unlucky now.

The new woman was as different from Ada Mae as could be. All hard, sharp angles where Ada Mae was soft curves. A slash where Ada Mae was a comma. All about herself where . . . You can see where I'm going with this. I didn't like her. No, it was more than that. I distrusted her, feared her, even hated her. That simple sentence, true as it may be, will take me weeks in confession to work out, no matter what penance the priest gives me. Perhaps confession won't help and it'll have to work itself out the way a splinter does from the bottom of a person's foot, leaving a scar that no one can see but the body always feels.

That woman. She had a name, though it took me till the wedding to discover it. Even then the town clerk mangled it so badly in the ceremony that none of us quite knew what to call her. The name was a mouthful and foreign: Constanza Reina Maria Barganza. Tom Morton called her that Con woman, which stuck. You'd think with a name like that she'd have been a Catholic, but she refused to set foot in church, not mine or any of the others. Like a near man with a dollar, she kept the coins of her religion close and let none of us know what they were until it was far too late.

I asked the priest and he said, "Fallen away, most like," meaning she'd been a Catholic once but chose a different

. . . .

66

path. A personal choice, and one I would have understood if only she'd owned up to it. But she didn't. She didn't own up to anything, leastwise to me.

And that wedding—a farce from beginning to end. There was no love, no cherishing, no obedience, no promises, no hope in it anywhere. All I could do was to hold Summer's hand and let her know I was always there if she needed me. Strangely, she pulled away from me, so I had to hold on for both of us. But I did indeed hold on.

· · · · · · · ·

PHOTOGRAPH

n their wedding picture, Step-
mama is in a white suit. She
said a long white dress reminded
her of a winding sheet, meaning grave clothes. Mama had
worn her wedding dress in her
coffin and the baby my old
christening gown. Shivering at the thought, Papa had agreed.

Not a hair out of place, Stepmama stares out at the
camera. Her hands clasp each other in a way that shows

· · · · · · · ·

off the simple gold wedding band she'd purchased herself. Her mouth is parted in a smile, but she doesn't look particularly happy. She looks hungry, a mountain lion ready to pounce. That was about the time I heard Miss Caroline whisper, "She wants the earth and moon with two strands of bob wire around it," and Miss Amelia adding, "And it whitewashed." At that, Cousin Nancy turned around and held her finger to her lips, shushing the two of them. But that was after the picture had already been taken.

Papa looks hungry, too, only not like an animal, but hungry the way a starving man looks hungry: hopelessly and helplessly. His head is turned away from the camera, and he's gazing at Stepmama's face. He's wearing his only suit, and one side of the collar of his white shirt is curling over, as if trying to get away from him, as if ready to fly to somewhere happier.

Off to the side stands Cousin Nancy, holding my hand and looking like she's fearing I'm the one—not Papa's shirt collar—trying to fly away. She's in her navy churchgoing suit, which makes her look dowdy and sad.

My pink dress with its heavy smocking, new bought by Stepmama for the wedding, shows up only as dirty white in the photograph. I'm glancing down at my new shoes because they're scuffed and I know already I'll have

· · · · · · · ·

to answer to Stepmama for that later. She's very particular about such things. She has told me that how a woman carries herself on every part of her person is magic. So, each scuff will mean a separate tongue-lashing. And another piece of hard work traded for betraying Stepmama's generosity. Of course after each scolding, I will get hugs and cold kisses. In those days I would eagerly take the tongue-lashing just to have those.

·10·

CHORES

or the longest time I didn't begrudge doing chores for Stepmama. Hadn't Cousin Nancy and I tackled the gardens during the time Papa was so buried in his grief? Hadn't we worked stooped over day after day? Children in those days worked hard both indoors and out. If I was doing different things for Stepmama, it was simply a part of the work we all did on the farm.

· · · · · · · ·

Stepmama worked hard, too. In fact, she took infinite care with Papa, feeding him up, making him his "*po*-tency drinks," as she called them. And at first he seemed to thrive under her care.

I watched as into the mortar she would put the leaves and seeds she'd brought with her, grinding them fine. All her concentration was on the work, and her tongue, like a little cat's, every now and then slipped out between her thin lips and moistened them. When she was satisfied at last that the mixture was as fine as it could get, she poured it into a glass canning jar and mixed it with fresh apple juice.

I reasoned, as an eleven-year-old does, that the drink wouldn't hurt a grown-up. Only a child. It must be—I told myself—like strong coffee, which, Cousin Nancy said, "when made right could float an iron wedge." But I thought it smelled and tasted more like the iron wedge itself. A rusted iron wedge.

Or maybe, I thought, *the po-tency drink is more like the moonshine the Morton cousins make and then drink until they act silly. But us kids are never allowed a bit of it.*

After a while, Stepmama let me do the grinding, though she measured out the amounts. That way I never touched them.

Stepmama, I told myself, *is just keeping me safe. That's what* real *mothers do.* Though of course since I was seven,

· · · · · · · ·

I'd little enough knowledge of *real* mothers except what I read about in the fairy stories, where stepmothers and grandmothers and even fairy godmothers don't always show up in the best of lights.

Certainly I couldn't have sworn then that Papa was hurt by the apple concoction. Just that he became distant from the moment he began drinking it, no longer responding to any of my questions. Not hugging me, even when I hugged him first. And of course he didn't sing again except in my dreams, though to be fair, he hadn't actually sung to me in years.

But he was still a powerful man. Didn't he go out into the gardens every morning and work until dark, Stepmama bringing him out the lunch she'd made with her own hands, so he didn't have to stop to come inside?

And didn't his heart still beat strongly? I could feel it pounding away when I snuggled into his lap of an evening, putting one of his arms over my shoulders like a woman adjusting a shawl. At these times a strange smile would flit across his face, like a mule eating saw-briars. Then his mouth moved as if to speak, though not a word fell out. And he'd shuffle his feet as a hound does, chasing after a deer or a rabbit in its dreams. It felt at those moments as if Papa was coming back to me when he was really moving on to a farther place.

· · · · · · · ·

•

After a full summer of this, even I couldn't ignore the fact that Papa was a changed man. Here and gone. Here and gone.

"What's wrong with him?" I finally asked Stepmama. It was on one of those wind-driven, rainy days when I couldn't go outside to play and Papa couldn't go outside to work in the garden and so he sat dozing in his big chair, fretting in his sleep.

She sighed. "Child, child, he's growing old is all!"

I knew he wasn't *that* old. Pop Wilber, the sawyer who lived up the nearest holler, was old. Nearly ninety, he still chopped wood for a living. Miss Skidmore, who lived a little way farther along, was eighty-seven and she still made quilts that won the top prizes at the county fair. Papa wasn't like them, white-haired, with lines like cursive writing up and down their faces. He didn't walk hunched over. His hands weren't all crabbed and cramped with time.

Papa was just distant. And increasingly strange.

But perhaps, my traitor's mind thought, *no stranger than he was after Mama died.* At least now he stayed home instead of running off to the churchyard every evening. At least now I could sit on his lap and he didn't throw me off.

Sometimes Stepmama led him by the hand out into the herb garden and sat him down on the wooden bench. Then

. . . .

she'd bend over and whisper in his ear as if she was aiming to have a conversation only with him. I could see her mouth moving as I sat by the kitchen window doing my homework. But what she whispered to him, I didn't know. And didn't dare ask. He rarely answered her; the few times he did, she would shake her head and her face got puckered like an old peach and her beauty fell away so that even I could see she was a different woman from what she ordinarily showed the world.

I should have relaxed, what with Stepmama taking care of Papa and her spending time talking to me and showing me how to grind things in her big mortar—nuts, herbs, flowers. Giving me hugs each time I did a good job. Calling me a beauty and a smart child.

However, little things made me wary. For instance, Papa stopped taking care of himself. His beard grew out long and scratchy, and I didn't want to sit on his lap anymore, or even rub his head, or come close, because he also began to smell. He smelled of unwashed bed linen and pee. He smelled musty, like a closet that's never been aired out. He smelled like the old stuffed bear at the hotel in Addison, the one that stands on its hind legs eight feet tall in the front greeting hall.

· · · · · · · ·

When Papa's hair began to flop down across his face, Stepmama herself cut it short with a fierce-looking pair of silver shears she'd brought with her. She put a bowl over the top of Papa's head to help shape the haircut, though she left his beard as it was, long and flecked with gray. And then for weeks he didn't look like Papa till the hair on his head grew back again. By then he was as shaggy as an old beggar man.

Old. Beggar man.

Old.

Maybe Stepmama was right. Papa was growing old even as we watched. And there's not much a person can do about that.

Strangely, Stepmama didn't throw away the hair she cut from Papa's head. I watched her stick it in her apron pocket, and then later on saw it on her mirror table in a little blue bowl the color of a robin's egg when I went in to get her bed linen for washing and airing. I was only in her room because she was out hanging up shirts on the line, which was too high for me to reach, and grumbling about it like always though she could have just tied the line a little bit lower down. I didn't tell her that. She'd sent me in to fetch the sheets and truth to tell, I was glad to go into her room. It drew me in as if I'd been pulled toward it with a magnet. We'd studied magnets in school that past year in science.

. . . .

I stared at the little bowl and tried to think why anyone would keep Papa's hair.

Maybe, I thought, *it's because she loves him so much she can't bear to be parted from even the smallest part of him.* I'd already seen how Papa was when Mama passed away. Grown-ups just acted different than kids. Different in unfathomable ways. Crazy ways. Just like they were tetched in the head. So, keeping someone's hair in a bowl was just another mad adult thing to do.

I put my finger into the bowl and stirred the hair around. There was a buzzing sound in the room as if bees had gotten in, and I suddenly got a short, sharp shock that ran up my finger, up my arm, up to the roots of my own hair.

I turned and ran out of there screaming without collecting the sheets and once I stopped hollering, I had to tell Stepmama what had happened.

She grabbed me by both arms and instead of giving me a hug and telling me there was nothing wrong and I was just fine said, "If you cannot go into my room without touching things, Snow, then you shall not be allowed to go into the room at all."

And for a year I didn't.

Wouldn't.

Couldn't.

My heart wouldn't let me. Nor would my legs.

. . . .

When people came to call—it was a very small town after all and everyone wanted to meet the new woman if only to talk about her when they'd left—Stepmama would go over to Papa and whisper something in his ear. Then Papa would suddenly leap up and about, almost laughingly so, dancing and joking and calling Stepmama by a dozen different names like "Honey" and "Sweetsop," and once even by my dead mama's name, Ada Mae. Though right after they left, he'd flop back in the chair, dreaming through the rest of the day.

Tetched, the both of them, I tell you.

Cousin Nancy didn't remark on Papa's condition directly to me, but some of the ladies in church did when she brought me to Christmas service, the one time that year Stepmama couldn't find an excuse for me to stay home.

"Well, I *never* . . . ," Miss Caroline said over my head, her one good eye all but sparking fire. "That man was so animated, why, it's like he'd been drinking all day long, though I thought he was teetotal. Mourning can sometimes take a man that way."

"Lem is not teetotal, though he rarely drinks," Cousin Nancy told her. "And certainly not to excess. And he's no longer mourning, he's married."

· · · · · · · ·

"Well, he surely was *animated*," Miss Caroline repeated, the fire in her good eye now banked.

And her sister, Miss Amelia, added, "Itchy, I'd have said." She pursed her lips.

"Itchy and odd," Miss Caroline shot back.

"No odder than before, going up that mountain all the time and . . ."

And from the other side, Miss Mae Morton, Papa's old cousin, with white hair that was so patchy her pink scalp showed through in places, looked straight at me. She lifted her finger, it all crooked from the arthritis, and said warningly, "Little pitchers . . ."

I knew what that meant. "Little pitchers have big ears." Meaning me. Meaning I would probably report back to Stepmama every word I heard. Only I wouldn't, though how were they to know?

At that warning, they all four sat straight-backed in the pew and began to sing "Away in a Manger" at the top of their lungs and all on different but interesting keys.

Cousin Nancy held tight to my hand, her face flushed and her hand much too warm around mine. I suppose I'd become accustomed to Stepmama's cold hands by then.

I kept thinking about how warm Cousin Nancy seemed as the priest droned on and on in his Christmas sermon,

· · · · · · · ·

talking about heresies and Pharisees and the like, none of which I quite understood except that they all happened a long time ago. All the while, Cousin Nancy was like a regular furnace. I felt almost burned up sitting beside her.

Then, when the congregation began to sing, I realized I'd forgotten the words of most of the carols. My neighbors seemed sudden strangers. All I had was Stepmama now. I shuddered and felt cold. Cold was comfortable. Cold was common. Cold was what I'd become used to.

Afterward, Cousin Nancy delivered me home from church, lifting me over the heavy snow plowed against the curb. Stepmama was waiting at the door, scowling, her arms crossed over her chest.

"Been long enough," Stepmama commented. "I've been *that* worried. Lemuel has been asking after her and I didn't know what I could tell him."

"Tell him Merry Christmas," Cousin Nancy said, smiling sweetly, but there was tartness in her tone.

"Thank you," Stepmama said to Cousin Nancy, as if suddenly remembering her manners. "I'm certain Snow had a good time."

"Summer certainly did," Cousin Nancy countered.

I remember thinking that it sounded like some kind of contest between them, their own version of the Europe

· · · · · · · ·

War. I didn't quite understand it then, except that it made me uncomfortable.

Once Stepmama closed the door firmly behind us, I asked why she'd said I had had a good time.

"Form," she answered. "Give them little to complain of. *Did* you have a good time, Snow?"

Suddenly I was not sure and took a while in answering. I had to think about the day in church. About how strange everything had seemed. How overly warm Cousin Nancy had been.

"I *think* so," I said at last.

If she heard something else in my answer, she kept it to herself, but the scowl was gone. She looked satisfied, a snake just swallowing its kill.

Remember, I was eleven. Stepmama was all I had, the only one who paid the slightest bit of attention to me every single day. I thought that made her a good person, only just someone not able to give any more than that little. That little had become enough.

For a while.

In fact, when we got inside, Papa didn't look a bit anxious. He was sitting in his chair, staring at the wall, though he could just as easily been on a far shore gazing at a horizon

. . . .

he never expected to reach. His face, always long and a bit mournful-looking even when he'd been young and happy, seemed extra long now. Bony. He stared out of eyes that looked encased in bone.

Old, I thought, and reached out for Stepmama's hand.

•11•

PAPA SINGS

 week or two later, I woke in the middle of the night and heard a strange sound, like a buzzing or humming. I tiptoed to my door and pulled it open. It hardly creaked at all.

The sound was coming from the living room and when I got halfway down the hall, I realized it was Papa. He was half singing, half chanting, and little of it made sense.

· · · · · · · ·

"I am the Green Man, the growing man, my mouth full of leaves," he said. "I wake in the spring, am reaped in the fall, slumber all winter dreaming of green." And then he sang out, his voice clear as in the past,

> *"Do I live for Summer or die for Snow?*
> *I cannot say. I do not know."*

I was about to go in when I heard Stepmama say, "Oh, for God's sake, Lemuel, stop that caterwauling!"

And then the sound of a slap, and Papa stopped.

Did I run in to protest? Or run back to my room in fear? I know what Molly Whuppie would have done. What Gretel would have done. What Janet who loved Tam Lin would have done. But I just stood there stock-still, listening.

Papa began again but in a softer voice, little above a whisper:

"I curl like a fiddlehead, sprout like a ramp, rise tall as corn. How green I am. Green as grass, as leaf, as stem. All, all green."

And then he sang:

> *"Get your beans, green beans, and gold,*
> *I am a has-bean, so I'm told."*

· · · · · · · ·

Another loud slap and then Stepmama must have gone back into their bedroom because I heard the door slam.

Only then did I tiptoe into the living room. And there was Papa in front of a blazing fire, dressed only in his nightshirt, dancing.

"Papa?" I whispered. "Are you all right?"

He turned around and stared at me, through me, and said quite clearly, "Green. That's it. Green. I am the Green Man, the growing man, my mouth full of vines and leaves. I wake in the spring, am reaped in the fall, slumber all winter dreaming of green."

And then he sank down onto the hearth and fell fast asleep.

I couldn't move him, so I just lay down by his side and—listening to his soft snores—finally fell asleep myself.

Stepmama must have been worried about Papa, though, for the very next day she sent for Doc McCorry, a scruffy old man with trembling hands, near to retirement.

Doc McCorry scratched his thinning hair and pronounced himself baffled, and after two more visits and a lot of prescribed tonics to Stepmama, he never came back.

Did I believe something bad was happening? Of course. Papa was clearly sick, fading away. Did I believe that Stepmama was the bad thing happening? Not for a moment.

. . . .

·12·

MIRROR, MIRROR

he day of my twelfth birthday, everything changed. Cousin Nancy was to come over to take me out for my treat. Stepmama had allowed it, but only begrudgingly. I thought it was that she distrusted Cousin Nancy's motives. That she wanted me close. Now, I believe, she just wanted me out of the house.

Everything I'd done that week had annoyed her—the clothes not washed clean enough, soft enough, fast enough.

· · · · · · · ·

The greens in the garden bolting with the heat and me not quick enough to bring them in. Three jars of canned apple jam exploding in the root cellar and the smell of it making her stomach turn, even after I'd mopped it all up.

And when I'd reported back to her after doing all the cleanup, she dismissed me, saying, "You look like you've been rode hard and put up wet," just as if I was an old horse. I must have given her a particularly miserable look, I was so hurt, it being my birthday and all. But she sent me to my room for sassing her, which I never did.

I grabbed up the little shard of mirror, which was all I had, and stared at myself. Who was this pinched, hungry-looking child? Maybe Stepmama was right. My face was white and pasty, my hair needed washing. There was a smudge over my right eyebrow. Anger was scribbled across my forehead. Once as bright blue as Mama's, my eyes now seemed bleached out, like a winter sky.

Of course Stepmama was angry with me, and not just for being too slow or too fast, for sassing her. She was a handsome woman and deserved a pretty stepdaughter. And Cousin Nancy was going to feel the same. So I did something I hadn't done in a year. Once Stepmama was off at the beauty shop, having her hair shagged and her brows plucked, I went into her bedroom though I'd long since been warned off.

. . . .

A year older—I thought—*and a year bolder,* like the girl in one of my favorite fairy tales, "Mr. Fox." In that story the girl sneaks into Mr. Fox's house—the strange man who'd been wooing her—where there is a saying carved over the door: *Be bold, be bold, but not too bold.* So being a little bit bold, I went right in, forgetting the rest of the story with its vats of blood and skin and bones because it's what Cousin Nancy calls a "cautionary tale" about walking out with wicked, murdering men, something no girl in her right mind would ever do, though lots seem to do it in the fairy tales.

I rummaged around in Stepmama's drawer of beauty aids and found some powder in a pink flowered box. I touched the powder lovingly with one finger. It puffed up into the air, as sweet as roses. I spread some on my cheeks and chin, rubbing it deeper until my skin seemed to tingle.

There were scents in bottles with rubber puffers. I tried three of them, one right after another, till I must have smelled like a meadow gone mad. And then, finding a rouge pot with a rosy-colored substance, I scrubbed color into one cheek and then the other.

The big mirror was covered with a black velvet cloth and I twitched it aside to take a look at myself. Expecting my own image to stare back at me, I was surprised. The mirror was so cloudy I could see only a large, filmy mass in the center of the glass. How could Stepmama possibly do her face while gazing into that cloudy old thing?

I leaned forward until my nose touched against the mirror's surface and a big splodge of powder rubbed off onto the glass.

"Oh, oh," I whispered, trying to rub it clean with my hand, which only made things worse. Stepmama would surely know I'd been in there. I turned to go out of the room and get some water to clean it off before she came back home.

"Oh, oh," the mirror said behind me.

I jumped and spun around, stunned, and as I did so I overturned one of the scent bottles. It crashed to the floor, spreading its oils everywhere.

"Who *are* you?" I asked, my voice tight, the broken bottle and the powerful smell ignored.

"Who are *you*?" the mirror responded.

"Snow," I said. "Snow in Summer."

"Snow in Summer," the mirror said, "ask and I will answer."

"Ask what?"

The cloudy mass grew larger, filled the mirror from side to side. "Is that your question, Snow in Summer?"

. . . .

"No. No. No." I knew the fairy tales. Mama had read them to me. Papa had sung them to me. Cousin Nancy had given me the books. I still regularly took a fairy-tale book to bed, reading till I fell asleep. I knew the stories by heart. Oh yes, I knew all about magic mirrors. The wicked queen in "Snow White" had one. And I knew all about magical questions, too. I would get only three of them. They shouldn't be wasted or I would end up with a sausage on my nose—or worse.

Did I wonder if the mirror was some trick that Stepmama had set up to catch me in her room?

Not even for a minute.

Did I think that this was some awful witchcraft?

It seemed too harmless for that.

A game perhaps?

I gave this a great deal of thought. Questions—ten of them, even a hundred of them—spun about in my head: questions about Papa's health, about Stepmama's desires, about Cousin Nancy's heart. Questions about who I was and what I would be when I grew up. Questions about whether Jimmy McGraw, who was in my class, liked me or if Wally Shaver, who was a year ahead of me, liked me better.

But at last I settled on the one question I most wanted an answer for. It was not a question that could possibly have a *good* answer. Still, I had to ask it.

. . . .

"Mirror," I said carefully, "will I ever see Mama again?"

The great mass in the mirror changed into a mask of a face, not a real one. There were no eyes, just a dead, black space where eyes should have been. The mask smiled, or rather the sides of the mouth turned up, which was not at all comforting.

"Yes," the mirror said.

"Yes," I whispered back.

The mirror paused, then in a different, deeper, more thoughtful tone said:

> *"You will see your mother twice, tears and laughter,*
> *But you will not know her until . . ."*

The door behind me opened with a great whooshing sound and Stepmama, newly shorn and polished, pounced on me, screaming, "Ungrateful child, hideous imp, you have touched what is mine without permission. You shall be punished for this . . . for this plundering."

The mirror whispered, "Long, long after."

They both spoke the truth.

The punishing times quickly followed. They began with a spanking, hard and fast with the back of the hairbrush on my bottom for the mess I'd made of her dressing table.

· · · · · · · ·

91

And for the broken scent bottle. And for using her powders and paints without permission. A spanking, and me twelve years old, practically a teen. It seemed horribly unfair. And absolutely right.

Nothing was said about the mirror. Stepmama probably didn't think me capable of asking it any questions. And she'd been shouting so loud, I'm sure she never heard it speak. In return, I didn't tell her what I'd seen. Or what I'd asked. Or what I'd heard. Besides, I was too busy howling to say anything.

When finally the spanking stopped and the howling stopped, I cried out, "It's my birthday."

"Double digits always are a bother," Stepmama said, as if she'd had children of her own and knew this already. I thought that if she'd had any, she'd probably drowned them like unwanted puppies at birth.

She made me clean the room while she stood over me, made me sop up the floor with my new birthday dress, a moss green one with little matching ribbons for my hair that Cousin Nancy had sent over.

And then she forced me to toss the ruined dress into the burn barrel while standing out behind the house in my underthings for all of Addison to see. I had to light the barrel, too, with matches she doled out one at a time, until

· · · · · · · ·

the contents caught fire. Though my face felt as if it had broken into a thousand pieces, my heart lay frozen in my chest. The dress went up in flames, until the bits of it rose up into the air like filthy dark green fireflies, filling the air until there was nothing left.

Next I had to write a letter saying I wouldn't be going out for my birthday, this one or the next, a letter dictated by Stepmama. And then I had to tack it to the front door for Cousin Nancy to find.

Lastly, Stepmama forced me to sit silently by the door and listen as Cousin Nancy found the note with her name on it. Listen while she opened it, read it out loud in a small whispery, weeping voice. Yes, I could hear her weeping and hear as she walked away how she said my name.

I didn't dare call out to comfort her for Stepmama had warned, "If you do any such thing, there will be nobody left alive in the house by nightfall to look after your papa."

Did I believe her?

Oh yes, I believed her.

Did I obey her?

Absolutely.

After all, she was punishing me for the bad things I'd done. And I *had* done them. I'd gone into her room, touched her private pots and paints and scent. I'd broken

. . . .

bottles on her floor. There were no excuses. It was her right to punish me. I was a sneak. An ungrateful child. No credit to my dead mama or fading papa.

So I believed her and obeyed her. I was just twelve years old. What other choice did I have?

And did I ever go into her room to speak to the mirror again? Not for a very long time. Fear—of both Stepmama and the mirror—kept me from it. After all, the daily punishments for that one mistake reminded me to stay away till it was almost too late.

The abuses came every day or two for weeks, all for infractions that only Stepmama noticed.

I ate too slowly or too fast. I ate with my mouth open, or not open enough. I didn't answer her in full sentences. I kept the light on in my bedroom to read at night. I cuddled with Papa, even when he didn't respond to me. I didn't do what she asked. Or I didn't do it quick enough. I left the door open, or closed it. I used too much water or too little. I forgot some chore.

And worst of all, I think, was that I didn't cry. Not when she hit me again with the hard side of the brush or with the bristle side or with the ruler I used for homework or a wooden clothes hanger or a ladle whenever the mood

· · · · · · · ·

took her, though she was always careful not to raise a bruise where anyone could see.

And I didn't cry when she made me stand out in the garden, nearly naked, where a person walking by—even kids from school—might catch a glimpse of me in my underthings.

Nor when she forced me to scrub the kitchen floor with my toothbrush.

Nor when I had to rake out the still-warm coals from the stove with my fingers.

Nor when she gave me only the scraps left over from her dinner.

No, the only time I wept was late at night in my bed, when I was certain she was asleep and not standing silently at the door listening. Every night for a week, a month, two months, three . . . until it all seemed normal and proper that I should be treated that way.

Was my spirit broken? I no longer had a spirit to break.

· · · · · · · ·

·13·

STEPMAMA REMEMBERS

hen I first apprenticed to the Master, I worked hard, both day and night. He taught me little in those first months but the value of hard work. Not the Craft, which was all I wanted. Instead I swept floors, scrubbed counters, set out potions and flowers and seeds whose names I didn't know and whose secrets I couldn't figure out on my own.

· · · · · · · ·

When I was too slow, he hit me. When I was too slip-shod, he yelled. He used a belt and a switch and a ruler on my knuckles, though I understood what he was doing and never complained.

And when he thought my spirit broken, and I biddable enough, he began to teach me down in the cellar, but only the smallest bits of the Craft.

He showed me how to tease out the future from an apple peeling, how to make a witch cake, how to curse a cow. He taught me skin on skin how to use my body as a gift, as a tool, as a weapon. He taught me giving and withholding. But the Deep Magicks he kept from me, and when I asked, when I begged, he looked at me crookedly and said formally, "When you are ready and not before."

He meant when *he* deemed me ready. I didn't want anyone—and certainly not any man—to have that power over me. And yet he had that power and more for I had fallen in love with him. That awful, gut-wrenching, knee-weakening love that makes true what is false, and mockery of any wish to be strong.

Finally, when he believed me ready, he taught me some of the Deep Magicks. How to poison and how to heal. How to put to sleep and how to awaken. How to strengthen and how to take away strength. He taught these to me by doing them *to* me. So I sickened and got well, died and came to life again. Over and over he did these things to me until I understood them down to my very bones.

I learned well and forgot nothing. I didn't have to write down the secrets, though I did so in a code of my own devising. But I had them secured in my head and knew I'd never forget a bit of what he taught me.

Then one day, when the Master had stayed out late into the night and came home to sleep in a stupor marked by his dark rattling snores, I decided I'd both the time and knowledge to do some snooping. Only I didn't call it that, of course; I called it "some growing" and "some learning" and "some searching for enlightenment." But calling a pig a princess doesn't lift it out of the sty. I was *snooping* all right, sneaking and stealing secrets. I was marking territory like a dog in its yard. And I was coming into my own.

Off to the side of the main cellar room where the Master had taught me most things was a small room, but it was always kept locked. Master wore the key to the lock around his neck and never let me in, not even to clean, though he went there whenever he felt like it and locked the door behind.

Aren't forbidden doors the most alluring? The old stories point that out surely. Even the greatest heroes and heroines fall under the spell of a locked door. And so did I.

· · · · · · · ·

98

That room—I was sure of it as I was sure of anything—held the final secrets of the Craft. The ones that would make me a Master in my own right.

I had managed to get an impression of the key as I toweled Master dry after a long, leisurely bath. Not trusting any locksmith with my desire, I'd made the key myself, pouring molten silver into a mold I'd created in secret. It had lain in my jewelry box, in a hidden compartment. And I waited—oh, I am good at waiting—till it was the hour of my fulfillment.

Checking once more that the Master slept the sleep of the not-quite dead, I crept down to the cellar, took out the silver key, and opened the door of the forbidden room. It squawked at the intrusion. I hesitated, ready to shut it quickly and be at work in the main room should I hear his steps on the stairs. But then once again his stentorian snores from two floors above floated down the stairs. I pushed open the door completely and went in.

There I found three things that I knew at once I had to make mine.

The first was a book of secrets written in a large readable hand that even a child could pick out. Master had no need of writing in code. He had never expected anyone but himself to ever read his magic book.

The second was a stone mortar, the pestle exactly fitting my hand. The Master's hand, with its swollen knuckles,

· · · · · · · ·

must have had a hard time using it. But the pestle might have been made especially for me.

And the third was a mirror covered by a dark cloth.

When I twitched the cloth off, there was a face in the glass, but not my own face. No, it was more a mask than a human likeness. It asked me my name and once I had said it—all my names, not just the one the Master called me—it told me to ask a question. After sorting through a dozen questions, I had about made up my mind when the door behind me swung open with a scream and Master was there.

His punishments were swift, but not swift enough. Nor harsh enough. I had already memorized two of the enchantments in the book, the one that saved my mind from harm, and the other that showed me how to kill a man without anyone knowing, not even the Master himself. And I used them both, willingly and with complete understanding of what I was doing.

So how could I let this silly child, this *Snow in Summer*, think to best me? Me, who had bested the Master?

Yes, I punished her. I had to. I could show her no mercy. At least not for a while. I liked it that she was strong enough not to cry. It made the game even more interesting. If it turns out she's a good foil, would make a fine apprentice, comes to the Magic willingly, then the seven years I take from her will be sweet and strong, like good wine.

· · · · · · · ·

But if she balks, if she refuses my offer—as her father has, fighting my green magic with his own—well, she'll make a lovely victim as well. The heart of a child new come to her womanhood, when stewed in cherries and brandy, is a powerful charm. If she won't give me the seven years of new life, she will at least give me that.

After several months of punishments, and the summer gone by, I let Snow think I was weakening. I even let her have a late birthday outing with her silly, puling Nan. It was an old trick but a good one.

For the moment, she's a useful tool: biddable, hard-working. As I was once for my Master. Besides, a girl's first blood course is the best time for the most potent of the Master's spells. Of course, if she must be killed, I can't do it directly myself. Small towns make that deed—however tantalizing—too chancy. It might even rouse her papa from his befuddlement, which I can't have. Or Cousin Nancy from her fear, though that is unlikely. I will have to be discreet. After all, the Craft is a subtle occupation, and I have much time ahead to figure out a promising plan.

· · · · · · · ·

·14·

A PRESENT

 was not sure when my sixth-grade teacher, Miss Alison, first noticed the burn marks on my fingers or the way my hair was often unplaited or unwashed. She was new in our three-room schoolhouse, a woman of quick smiles and a chirrupy voice, like a sparrow in human form. How was she to know what I'd been like before?

But even she in her sparrow way figured out something was wrong. Perhaps one of the children pointed it out. Or one of the parents who'd known Papa before.

She sent for Stepmama to come in to talk about how poorly I was doing in school. The two of us stood before her, me with my head down, like a student wearing a dunce cap. Stepmama stared Miss Alison straight in the face as if *her* conscience, at least, was clear.

"Miss Curtin told me before she left that Summer was her star pupil, bright and sunny, eager to learn," Miss Alison chirruped. "Said Summer was the one child she'd miss following her retirement."

"If *Snow* isn't doing well here," Stepmama said starchly, "then I'll teach her at home. She'll learn from me all that she needs to know."

We both heard the threat in that and Miss Alison answered quickly. "Oh, that won't be necessary, Miz Morton," she said. "I'm sure Snow in Summer will do well enough. I'll continue to encourage her. *Chirp. Chirp. Chirp.*" She took a little bird breath. "It would be a shame to"—here she stumbled—"to burden you further." She meant further than a husband who was fading into the woodwork. Further than a house that was falling down around our ears. A garden that was overgrown. A family

· · · · · · · ·

that dwelt in rumors. Further than a once-bright child failing at school.

And so the lines had been drawn. The war begun. But still the little princess lived in the tower with the dragon. There was nothing a chirrupy teacher could do about that. If I had hope of rescue, it wasn't going to come from Miss Alison. Or Cousin Nancy. Or Papa. Or any of the Morton clan.

If I was going to be rescued, I was going to have to rescue myself.

Yet, in a strange way, rescue did come from Miss Alison. Oh, not directly. And not all at once. But a week later, she bumped into Cousin Nancy at Cogar's meat counter, and they got to talking as neighbors will, and suddenly Miss Alison told her all. About the burn marks on my fingers, the deep circles under my eyes, the unplaited hair, and all the rest.

Cousin Nancy wrote out a paper in her careful hand stating her *can do's* and *must do's,* and then marched to our house that Sunday in her very best churchgoing outfit, a gray dress with white piping and a hat to match. She was carrying a big old brown leather satchel, which didn't match her outfit, and *that* made me wonder.

· · · · · · · ·

She knocked smartly on the door and when it was opened by Stepmama, Cousin Nancy spoke right up. She didn't start with any pretty words about how nice it was to see Stepmama or wasn't the autumn weather glorious or the usual slow greetings we have in Addison. No, Cousin Nancy showed backbone by coming right to the point. "I *am* taking Summer to church with me this morning."

Of course, she didn't expect to be greeted pleasantly and was prepared for the worst—at least the worst as she envisioned it—but Stepmama surprised her. Cocking her head to one side as if sizing up an adversary, Stepmama answered, "That's fine. I think Snow needs some moral schooling. She's become careless and sneaky. She covets my things, talks back to her elders, grows lax in her personal habits, and is failing at school."

"I never . . . ," I began, but remembered shamefully that I *had* sneaked into her room and I *had* broken her things, and I had spoken to the mirror about my dead mama, and I was definitely failing in school. Suddenly, I understood that from *Stepmama's* point of view, I was all the bad things she'd just said. I shut my mouth, hung my head, and waited for judgment.

Stepmama added, "I'll be taking her to my own church when she turns fourteen and have her baptized there."

. . . .

Cousin Nancy interrupted her. "She's already been bapti—"

Holding up a hand that silenced Cousin Nancy mid-word, Stepmama smiled that slow serpent smile. "She will be born again in my church, I promise you *that*."

I trembled, because the smile didn't match the promise. Or maybe I mistook the promise.

Stepmama took a short breath and continued, "In the meanwhile, you may see her for her birthdays. And on each Sunday you may take her to your church or Lemuel's. Which one is up to you. But I expect you to correct her lapses in moral judgment." She smiled again, this time at Cousin Nancy, but the smile never reached her eyes.

I was stunned, and certainly didn't trust that Stepmama had changed her mind about me, only her tactics. But even that wariness couldn't hold back the happiness that, like a warm blanket, folded around me.

Stepmama had given Cousin Nancy something.

Cousin Nancy counted it a victory.

As did I.

But oh, we were so wrong.

Cousin Nancy and I walked directly to her church without me even taking time to get into my churchgoing clothes in case Stepmama should change her mind and call me back.

· · · · · · · ·

"And that's not all, Summer," Cousin Nancy said. "After Mass we are going for a belated birthday celebration lunch at Cogar's soda fountain."

"But Stepmama won't allow it . . ."

"We're not telling Stepmama nor are we asking," she told me with more spunk than I'd heard from her in several years.

It put that same spunk in me. I squared my shoulders and walked with a more sprightly step.

"You're twelve now, and a few months more," Cousin Nancy said in her soft voice. "You've lived almost as long without your mama as with her." She said it as if telling me a secret, but it was a secret we both knew.

For a moment I considered telling her what the mirror had said to me about seeing Mama again. But what she said next stopped that confession cold.

"You'll see your mama in heaven someday. But until then, there are certain things she'd have me do for your protection. I'm your godmama after all." She took a deep breath. "Forgive me, child, that I've not done a good job of caring for you in the last year or so."

I didn't quite know how to think about that. She'd given me a fact of life and a fact of death squashed together. It was an uncomfortable place to be at twelve. And she'd made the

· · · · · · · ·

mirror's promise of seeing Mama once more nothing but a promise of life after death in heaven. That was not what I was hoping for, but some greater bit of magic from the mirror. Somewhat more subdued, I nodded and said nothing in return and soon enough the little Catholic church came into view.

Mass seemed both long and short. The priest—a circuit rider from Clarksburg—told some interesting stories, but their points were lost on me. I kept thinking about the fairy tale I'd read the night before in bed, about the good girl who spoke in diamonds and pearls, the bad girl in vipers and toads. Both seemed an uncomfortable gift. Either way, their own voices were lost.

Cousin Nancy and I sat silently side by side after his sermon. She was silent because she was praying hard; I was silent because I was afraid to break whatever spell had been cast. Also I was wondering how much I would have to pay for this moment of peace, and yet at the same time I was so happy to be there, I would have willingly given anything for it to continue.

Anything.

Then Cousin Nancy stood, to go down with the others who were taking communion. I knew I couldn't go with

. . . .

her because I hadn't been through the proper study. Step-mama's arrival into our lives had put a stop to that. Even if I could have done so, I was certain I hadn't lived a good enough life the past year to be allowed at the rail. I'd lied, coveted, didn't honor either father or stepmother, was full of greed. Just thinking about taking communion invited lightning to strike me down. When it didn't, I was less relieved than surprised.

Afterward, we walked back along the road toward Cogar's. Silence stretched between us. Cousin Nancy seemed wrapped in a kind of sanctity. I was still vibrating with my close call.

There at the town's second bottom, the single row of storefronts—Cogar's, the drugstore, Lawyer McAdams's office, and the doctor's office—all leaned together like old friends. It had been months since I'd been down that way. Stepmama kept me much too busy to even think of such an adventure.

Cousin Nancy had her arm tucked through mine, the way two women do when they stroll through town. I could feel her warmth coming in waves toward me. I hadn't been warm like this in a while. Far too long.

When we got to Cogar's door, Cousin Nancy said, "I have a present for you." She slapped her hand against the

· · · · · · · ·

brown leather satchel. "But you have to keep it from your stepmama."

I looked down at the ground and nodded before looking up at her. Cousin Nancy's green-gray eyes softened. She read my face and she got a misty look about her, which gave a luster to her familiar face, like washing old china till it sparkles, till you remember the good of it.

"I *will*," I said. "Oh, I will. I've kept other things from her." I hesitated, then added, "*Most* things."

"My strong girl," Cousin Nancy said, not asking me what those other things were in case I didn't want to say. "If only your poor papa could be so courageous. But of course that witch woman has him be-spelled."

Be-spelled. That certainly made sense to me.

We went inside and sat down at the counter.

"Give this child anything she wants," Cousin Nancy said to Mary Lou behind the counter, dressed in her blue-striped dress and big white apron.

"Anything?" Mary Lou asked. It was past wartime of course, and past the Depression, not that you could tell in West Virginia. There wasn't a whole lot of *anything* on offer.

Cousin Nancy nodded. "It's her twelfth birthday."

"Today?" asked Mary Lou.

"That's when we're celebrating it," Cousin Nancy said, which was—and wasn't—an actual lie.

· · · · · · · ·

I ordered a tuna salad sandwich and a bottle of pop. "This is the best present ever," I said to Cousin Nancy, the words garbled because I had shoved the sandwich into my mouth without regard for the manners Stepmama had been forcing on me. The sandwich was so much better than the scraps from Stepmama's meals, scraps that were all gristle or bone.

"Oh, the present is for later," Cousin Nancy said. "Out of sight of any eyes and ears but our own. This is just lunch."

"Little pitchers . . . " I said, and smiled a mouthful of fish.

Then Cousin Nancy touched the back of my hand. "No need to gobble it down, Summer. I'm happy to buy you a second one."

I nodded, slowed, began to savor the food. As for the bottle of pop—it was heaven. I ended up drinking another.

Cousin Nancy smiled back and whispered, "Mary Lou is more like a *big* pitcher."

We laughed companionably. It felt good to laugh.

Afterward, we went up the hill to the old salt sulfur springs and sat on a bench, the dark stink of the sulfur wrapping around us, making us all but invisible.

"Witches can't abide a good salt sulfur spring," Cousin Nancy said, "so your stepmama won't find us here." Whether it was true or not, I believed her.

. . . .

Then Cousin Nancy put her hand into the leather satchel and drew out a packet made of white tissue paper wrapped about with a sturdy brown string. Handing it to me, she said: "Happy birthday, Summer."

I opened the packet quickly, and a string of garlic and a rowan branch tumbled into my lap along with a little brown paper bag with rowan berries that Cousin Nancy must have been saving since last fall.

"What's this about?" It was certainly an odd thing to be given for a birthday present.

"The garlic is to ward off bloodsuckers and the rowan branch is proof against witches," she said. "Nail the garlic over your bedroom window, the branch over your bedroom door. Put the berries, just a few at a time, in your papa's pockets."

. I wondered how this squared with the teachings of the church. But here in Webster County, the old mountain ways were still followed even by the most ardent Christians.

"But surely she'll know . . ."

"Let her think that's all there is to it," Cousin Nancy said, her face crinkling up like an old peach too long in the sun. "Homey magicks." Then she pulled out an envelope from her bag and handed it to me. "This is the *real* present. You're gonna become a woman someday soon and will need it." She had a strange look I couldn't parse, like

· · · · · · · ·

a long sentence in a grammar lesson at school. "We must fight magic with magic, child."

"Magic," I whispered, and allowed myself to finally understand what I'd been battling.

I knew Cousin Nancy had little money, her being a widow and times still being hard. All she had was her government wages from the post office and the bit of Cousin Jack's pension from the army, so I hadn't expected a real gift. But the gift of understanding what I was up against was better than anything she could have bought me at a store.

"Open it carefully," she said, though the warning was unnecessary. Her gray-green eyes had a watery look. Like the Elk River running slow in summer.

Inside was a birthday card with a poem exhorting me to be a good child. And a photograph, one she said she'd found tucked away in one of her drawers. Staring out of the photo were Papa and Mama in their marrying clothes. They both looked stiff and scared and happy all at the same time, Papa so young and vital, I almost didn't recognize him. He stood tall and thin, like a boy who'd grown up too fast and his body hadn't quite caught up with the growing. His long face looked softer, fuller than ever I remembered it. And Mama, small and pretty, her hair in long dark braids, a dimple in her chin—the same as I have—stood straight by

· · · · · · · ·

his side, clutching his arm. Even in the picture you could see the strength in her hand, the knuckles near white, as if there was nothing that would make her let him go.

Nothing but death.

A second envelope sat within the first, crinkled like it had been handled too often. I touched it tentatively, then worried open a little bit of the flap. Inside was a single sheet of folded-over paper. Slowly I opened it and gaped.

A strange piece of grayish material, a bit like a cap with long rubbery ribbons, lay there. Along its edges, the paper had turned light brown, like a water stain. The whole cap was oddly puckered, almost a map of our town, the center surrounded by little peaks and valleys. I touched the thing tentatively but couldn't identify it.

"Your caul, child," Cousin Nancy said. "I retrieved it right after you were born. Salted it down, let it dry over the rim of a bowl. I've kept it for you all this time. I knew it'd be important for you to have it one day."

"What . . . what do I *do* with it?" I was afraid to touch the thing again. Just the thought of doing so made me a little sick.

"Just keep it on you. Always. As long as *she* lives there." Meaning Stepmama. Meaning in our house. Then Cousin Nancy reached into her pocket and pulled out a little drawstring bag. "Keep it in this, which bore the gift from your

· · · · · · · ·

dear mama to me when she asked me to stand as your god-mama. Keep the caul in this. It'll bring you luck. And, more important, it'll protect you."

Luck and protection. I certainly could use both, though neither of us said that aloud. I took the string bag and closed the horrible rubbery caul up inside it. Then, shuddering slightly, I put the drawstring over my head and tucked the bag under the front of my dress, where it made scarcely a bump or lump.

Then Cousin Nancy got out another bottle of pop that she'd stored in her satchel, plus two glasses. That satchel was like the never-empty bag in the tale about the old woman and the wind. I wondered what else it contained.

Filling each glass to the brim, Cousin Nancy told me the story of when I was born, a story I hadn't heard in years.

"Your mama was plumb wore out from your birth, but when she held you, all her spirit came flooding back into her." Cousin Nancy smiled. "She stared down at you lying by her side and said, 'Looky there, Nan, she's all red and white and black,' her voice a wonderment, though weak. 'Like that girl in the fairy tale.' Your mama just plain loved the old tales."

"Happily ever after," I said. "Anyways, that's the promise."

That made Cousin Nancy glow, like she was a jack-o'-lantern all lit up inside. She kept her hands tight clasped in

· · · · · · · ·

her lap, afraid to reach out and touch me in case I shrank back away from her like I had before. How could she have known that now I'd have welcomed that embrace? Even if I couldn't have told her so. But she said, like it was an echo, *"Happily ever after,"* and clinked her glass against mine.

We both knew Mama's story and my story were a long way from any such happiness. And at twelve, heading for adulthood, a child fears that the way she is at that moment is all she's ever going to be. *Un*happiness seemed to me a straight line into forever. I clutched onto the drawstring with all my might and made a birthday wish. Then I clinked her glass with mine.

When we walked back to my house, I believe that both of us were fearful that our faces would give away what had happened between us: a small hope if not an actual promise of happiness ahead. But Stepmama was gone, a note on the door stating only: *Gone to church.*

"Which church?" asked Cousin Nancy, for it was already three in the afternoon, way past time for any service in any of the churches around here.

"I don't rightly know since Stepmama hasn't ever been to any church that I know of," I said, shrugging. Then, putting my hand over my chest and feeling the horror/

· · · · · · · ·

comfort of the bag and what was in it, I opened the door and went inside.

Cousin Nancy didn't come in, of course. She hadn't set foot *inside* the house since the day Stepmama arrived. I waved at her out the window, then turned.

As always, Papa sat in his chair by the fire though it was unlit since this was still early fall. But he smiled just a bit at me, possibly more a touch of heartburn than an emotion. Still, I took it as a sign and after stuffing some of the rowan berries in his pants pockets, I gave him a huge grin and went into my room.

I glanced back right before closing my door. His head had already sunk back onto his chest and he'd begun to snore again.

Heartburn, then.

But the church thing was niggling at me. If Stepmama planned to take me along, I needed to know what to expect. There were all kinds of churches, up and down one side of our mountain and the next. Most of those churches were pure Baptist and some were Pentecostal and a few—a very few—were Catholic. I heard this from the kids at school. But none of them, as far as I knew, met late Sunday afternoon. So was she *really* at her church—or up to something else? And how would I ever find out?

· · · · · · · ·

It was too much of a dark puzzle for me and thinking about it threatened to spoil my joy in the day. So I put it out of mind and went into my bedroom. There I reread Cousin Nancy's card and looked at my parents' photograph for the longest time. Then I put them both in the secret drawer of my dresser. Next, I nailed the string of garlic over my window and the rowan branch over the door, believing that now I was as protected as I could be. And, I hoped, Papa, too.

I went back into the living room, carrying my homework with me, to watch Papa sleep until the night wrapped around the house. Only then did the front door open and Stepmama—like a shadow—slip back into the house, taking her scarf off as she entered and filling the house with cold.

·15·

COUSIN NANCY REMEMBERS

've often wondered about courage. Easy to read about it in the old tales, where it takes the right sword or spell to defeat the witch. Easy to read about it in scripture, where a good heart and a strong belief are all one needs to be armored against evil. But courage in this world is a subtler thing. A word said right or wrong.

· · · · · · · ·

A chance meeting. A photograph. A promise. A satchel. A caul.

Would any of these save my godchild from what lives in her house and attacks her soul? Would any of these save her from that she-devil's hand?

And what about my poor Lem, who is all but lost? Did I lose him or did he lose himself?

Yet take heart, Nan. Aren't we promised that the lost will be found, good turn away evil, the prodigal return? Doesn't the priest warn against sinking into despair, which is a lack of hope? Doesn't he tell us that losing hope is a sin?

I will *not* lose hope. I will find my small bit of courage so I can help Lem somehow find his.

That night, of the twelfth birthday lunch with Summer, when I got down by the side of my bed and said my prayers, I spoke for a long time to Ada Mae. I could just about see her at my bedside, wrapped in a flowing white robe, her white wings fanned out behind her, an angel.

"Ada Mae," I said, "help me that I may do God's work. And yours."

She smiled, but she said nothing.

I suppose angels don't talk to mortals simply because we want them to, but only under orders from God. So I stood up, realizing with a sharp pain under my breast that in fighting this thing, except for God's watchful eye, I was to be on my own.

But surely, I thought with a shiver, *that's enough.*
It had to be.

· · · · · · · ·

·16·

SIGNS

y courses came right before my thirteenth birthday, early for some, late for others, but my mama's had done the same, or so Cousin Nancy had warned me. The very next week, Stepmama told me we'd be off to church together on Sunday.

Since she'd said I was to go when I turned fourteen, I wasn't really prepared for it. But evidently, it was getting my first period that decided Stepmama that it was time.

· · · · · · · ·

By then I'd had over two years with Stepmama and should have been ready for anything. Two years of charms, cozening, threats, curses, cold comfort, privation. Two years of icy glares, small meals, hard work. Two years of watching Papa sink deeper and deeper into his chair despite my stuffing his pockets with the rowan berries any chance I got, mostly after I'd washed and ironed and hung his trousers in the cupboard. Still Papa slipped further away into the comfort of his chair till it was hard to tell which was which.

It's not for nothing they say around here: "Meanness don't happen overnight." Stepmama was well practiced in meanness. And the thing about meanness is, it saps the spirit. There were times when I felt like sinking deep in Papa's chair with him.

But at least the beatings had stopped. The pinchings, too. The garlic and rowan branch and caul had worked magic enough for that. And even though it may have had as much to do with my getting older and wiser and sneakier, I thought every day since: *Thank you, Cousin Nancy.*

I had taken to wearing the caul in its string bag around my neck, taking it off only when I bathed, and even then kept it close to hand. I'd made new little bags to house the caul; the best and safest was one I sewed in home ec class, under the watchful eye of Mrs. Cadwell. The bag was of

· · · · · · · ·

silk with silver and gold threads. And a few bits of Papa's hair that I stole out of the bowl on Stepmama's table.

Yes, I believed the caul had kept me safe. And maybe the thing was also somehow a sign from God. I began to believe that even if I couldn't ever best Stepmama, I could outlast her. I mean, I was almost thirteen and she was old. *Nigh on to thirty-five if she was a day,* I thought. Even her powders and face paint couldn't disguise the age lines and the gripe lines that ran as deep as the railway tracks some said were bound to cross our mountain any day soon. *A railway!* I longed to see one, but I knew Papa would hate it, the steel rails crushing the green.

As I got closer to my birthday, I promised myself that when I was old enough, I would run off and make my own life. Ride a train. Go to a city. Maybe even take classes at the university in Morgantown. It was all a dream, of course. At eight or nine or even ten and twelve, I could never dare to actually believe such a thing could happen. But with my thirteenth birthday looming, suddenly I *did* dare. And believing it, I was lulled into a sense of safety instead of constantly looking for a way out on my own.

My Sundays at church with Cousin Nancy and the everyday-ness of school, where I once again shone, seemed

· · · · · · · ·

enough to sustain me. Though I hadn't any close friends—because I'd no one I was allowed to spend time with after school—I wasn't bothered by it. The girls at school thought me stuck up, but it was more as if I was bottled up. I kept my heart and my confidences tightly locked away. As for the boys, they were intent on hunting and fishing and telling stupid jokes. The other girls laughed at them, but I couldn't do any such thing. So they ignored me as well.

At least by now I knew what to expect from Stepmama. Or I thought I did. Love—true or otherwise—was no part of the equation.

And then I woke on an ordinary school day at the hind end of May with blood on my sheets and a queasy stomach. I wasn't particularly surprised. I knew what I had to do.

Stripping the bed quickly so that the mattress wasn't spoiled, I washed the sheets by hand with lye soap and salt till my fingers were sore. Then I put the sheets through the wringer, careful not to get any of my fingers caught. Papa had a sprung thumb from the time he helped his mama with the wringer. I knew a moment's inattention could mean disaster.

Then I hung the sheets out to dry. This all before Stepmama woke. But since I always did the laundry before going to school, there should have been nothing about my washing the sheets to alert her.

. . . .

Cousin Nancy had already given me a copy of *Good Housekeeping* magazine at Christmas and pointed out the ads in it for Kotex. She even slipped me several of the napkins. I'd been a bit embarrassed by the present except she was so matter-of-fact about it. However, it turned out to be a fine gift because now I could take care of myself without letting Stepmama know. I'd hidden the napkins in my bottom drawer, under my winter nightgowns, a scattering of rowan berries on top—just in case Stepmama should pry.

So off I went to school that morning, with one of the napkins pinned in my panties, another two stuffed in my school satchel, thinking myself safe.

But Stepmama must have had a secret talent I hadn't been aware of. She sniffed out the blood even though those sheets—snapping in the May wind and glistening in the morning sun—smelled only of sunshine, lye soap, and salt.

When I got home, she was waiting for me, the bottom sheet in her hands. She didn't want to see the 100 percent I'd gotten on the arithmetic test or the A+ on the English paper that I'd labored over for three nights though usually that's the only part of my schooling she was interested in.

"So, you're a woman now," she said abruptly, holding up the telltale sheet, which to my eyes was white as snow, white as the name she called me.

· · · · · · · ·

"I'm thirteen. Almost. That's hardly a grown woman."

But it was merely her way of letting me know that *she* knew. And my snappish answer, usually bitten off before I ever dared speak it aloud, let her know all.

"On Sunday you'll come to church with me." She didn't touch me. She hadn't touched me since I'd come home from my birthday celebration wearing the caul around my neck. But there are subtler ways to practice abuse. "May's the perfect time to celebrate."

Perfect time for what? I wondered. *Celebrate what?* But I didn't ask. Instead, looking down at the ground, I asked, "Which church?"

I tried to speak casually, as if the question didn't matter, but she'd guessed in a moment. Smiling that serpent smile, she waited for me to look up and notice, and only then turned away.

It should have been a warning. It certainly was a sign. But I didn't recognize it until later. Much later.

Stepmama's church was far enough away that we had to drive to get there. It was rare that I was allowed in her car. I'd been in it only twice in my life, once when I'd had a toothache so bad my cheek swelled up to twice its size and I had to be taken to the dentist out in Cowan, fourteen

· · · · · · · ·

miles away; once when I'd had a tonsillitis attack that was so bad, Stepmama took me to the hospital in Richwood, over an hour on the twisting road.

If I'd been looking for signs, the weather was bright and the sky still shining, the color of apricots. The roads were clear as we made our way up the mountain. It was warm enough that we had the windows down. Anyone watching us might have thought they were seeing a girl and her mother driving off into the evening in companionable silence. A girl dressed in a modest long skirt, her mother with a face scrubbed clean of lipstick and powder and a navy blue scarf covering her hair. I thought it a peculiar way to dress for church. Cousin Nancy and her friends always wore their finest. But there we were, in the dowdiest of clothing, and Stepmama was looking decidedly unlike herself.

Well, at least the silence was real.

The night birds were already singing. One had a high-pitched squeak that sounded like a door that needed oiling: *Aek-aek, aek-aek.* And then the whip-poor-wills started up. I tried to pretend they were angels following me, just in case, but it was just the ordinary kind of birdsong you hear on a spring night.

Soon enough, I knew, the sky would be full of stars. Sometimes on the mountain, they seemed close enough to touch.

· · · · · · · ·

When we rounded the hairpin turn going out of town, the trees closed in overhead like curtains, and cold air suddenly rushed in through the open windows.

"Close your window tight," Stepmama said. It was to be the only thing she said to me until we reached the church.

We drove for maybe a half hour more along the curving road, then suddenly turned off the blacktop onto a country lane. Another few hundred yards and I saw an old building backed up against the tall, dark trees. Once upon a time it had probably been somebody's house, but now it had a plywood steeple tacked up over the second floor, the top of it reaching above the roof like a hand signaling for help.

There was something carved over the front door. As we got closer, I could read it: *With Signs Holy Church.*

I said the words out loud, then turned to Stepmama. "What does that mean?" But she didn't answer.

We drove nearly up to the church door, and I was afraid we were going to drive right in, but at the last moment she turned the wheel sharply and landed us up on the grass. There were about a dozen dark-colored pickups parked close by.

Only one man was outside the church, standing by the front door. He was sucking hard on a cigarette as if to get it all smoked down before the service began. When he

· · · · · · · ·

saw Stepmama, he let some of the smoke drift back out through his nose, suggesting a banked fire.

"We're here," said Stepmama to me.

I didn't say, "Obviously." Stepmama never said anything obvious. There had to be a reason that she told me. *Maybe an emphasis,* I thought. Like underlining something in an essay, which my teacher said was one way of letting the reader know you really mean something.

We got out of the car and walked to the door.

"Evening, Miz Morton," the smoking man said. "Things are about to start. Reverend Fred has some new—"

Stepmama stopped him with a hard glance.

"Some news," the man said, flicking away the cigarette. I watched as its little red light fell into the short grass like a shooting star. "He has some news."

I didn't think that was what he meant to say, but like Papa, he was under Stepmama's charm.

Now I could hear singing through the closed door. It was nothing like the singing in Cousin Nancy's church, which is quiet and often off-key. This was a rollicking, hand-clapping version of the old union song "We Shall Not Be Moved." I could feel the beat of it beneath my breastbone.

Suddenly touched by the song, I began humming along.

"Enough," Stepmama warned, hand raised.

. . . .

Even though I knew she wouldn't hit me—not while I was wearing the caul, and not in front of this man—I stopped humming.

She pushed through the door and we went in.

I was used to the beauty of Cousin Nancy's church with its simple pews and the single lovely stained glass window. Even the plain Baptist church I remembered going to with Papa—long before Stepmama came into our house and our lives—even that church was pretty compared to this. And the one time Mama had taken me into the abandoned church on the mountain, it was peaceful; the very stones seemed to breathe.

But here in With Signs Holy Church the main room was no more than two or three rooms of the old house knocked together, the walls separating them having been removed. I could still see where the old walls had been. The low ceiling made me feel pushed down, not lifted up as I did with the high vaulting of Cousin Nancy's church. Besides, I could see where the paint was peeling off. The curtainless windows were closed against the cold of the night. In fact, several of them had been painted over with black paint.

There was little in the church sanctuary but three rows of wooden benches, a long table at the front, and a stove

· · · · · · · ·

in a corner, already lit. It's not for nothing the mountain is nicknamed "Freeze Your Heart Mountain" and "the Ice Maiden." That stove was pumping out a stream of heat. A stack of cordwood lay right beside it and every now and then, one of the men would slip another log in.

On the walls were cutout magazine pictures of Jesus with his hands on the heads of different small children, all of them white, ragged, and adoring. Also three handmade quilted banners hung from the ceiling by ropes. One said: *Jesus Saves*. The second proclaimed: *Welcome to With Signs Holy Church*. The third stated simply: *Mark 16:16–18*. I was pretty sure that last referred to the Bible, but as to what verse I had no idea.

In one corner of the hall stood a knot of women, all of them maybe Stepmama's age or a bit older. They wore print dresses that came down well below their knees. The women chattered together though not in a prayerful way. More like crows cawing.

In another corner several men in overalls were huddled, talking in hushed tones, their hands making strange signs in the air.

Just then, four men marched in from a door at the back of the sanctuary, carrying wooden boxes they set down on the table in front of the benches. The boxes all had sturdy tops.

. . . .

There was no one my age at all in the church, though several boys who looked like they were already out of high school stood together in the far back, jawing. And one girl who might have been anywhere from fifteen to twenty, heavily pregnant, was a row behind us, pointedly not looking at any of the boys. Of course in those days, it wasn't unusual for mountain girls as young as fourteen to get married. My own mama had me when she was barely sixteen and she and Papa had been married for over a year at that point.

Every now and then, the boys looked over at Stepmama, and the tallest, blondest one nodded at her. He was handsome in a heavy-lidded way, his hair combed straight back to show off his broad forehead, which served to emphasize his eyes and those heavy lids. He tried to act as if he didn't know he was being watched, but of course the satisfied half smile gave him away.

Stepmama nodded back at him with one hand raised, and with the other, she pushed me toward the front of the room.

I could only wonder at this church and these people. However did Stepmama find it in the first place, and what possibly kept her coming back?

It was all terribly strange.

And about to get stranger.

. . . .

·17·

STEPMAMA REMEMBERS

ow we come to the moment that my plan unfolded. I had waited with the exquisite patience of the serpent. Snow would either accept me and the Craft, accept that I would take seven years from her life in exchange for knowledge, or she would die—but not at my hand. Her father would slip away in sorrow. The land would then become mine by marriage right, with no shares

· · · · · · · ·

to any other person alive. The dead have no rights in this country.

And with that money, I would find some other young person just on the cusp of adulthood. I was still a young woman myself. There was no rush yet. Master had made many servants of the Craft before me. I would make many in my turn.

And hadn't I earned my widow's portion these past few years, stuck out in this forsaken mountain town, tied to a man whose silent fight against my potions has all but maddened me; his daughter's small, insignificant rebellions only proving an irritation.

The mirror has promised me everything I asked for and more. Or at least it seemed that way:

"Wait until the time is right,
You'll have what's yours without a fight."

Days, weeks had gone by. I wondered if I had misread the answer.

But when I found the With Signs church, everything came together. Everything I wanted, I found in this one dismal place: fear and hope, rage and renewal, poison and antidote.

Liberty Lake Municipal Library
Washington

· · · · · · · ·

The boy teetering on manhood is my linchpin.

My stepdaughter just entering womanhood brims with magic and years.

I tremble in anticipation. The mirror has made promises. I will work to make them come true.

The serpents are to hand.

The serpents are to hand.

Hush—the charm's wound up.

Liberty Lake Municipal Library
Washington

·18·

MARK 16:16–18

didn't know why, but even in that hot room, I was shivering and on the edge of my seat as the preacher and two of the other men motioned everyone to sit. The preacher's two helpers drew up chairs from somewhere and sat on either side of the table where the wooden boxes had been set.

The man on the right had hair the color of a night sky, and the little black hairs on his well-scraped chin had

· · · · · · · ·

already started coming through again, like a shadow on his otherwise unremarkable face. The man on the left was his exact opposite, one of those white blonds we have throughout the county, his cheeks reddening noticeably in the heat of the room.

Then the preacher came around in front of the table, Bible in hand. He was a thin man with a long face, like a vulture's, and black, watery eyes. He nodded right and left at the members of his congregation but didn't say a word. There was something compelling about him, something that his congregation might have called holiness, but what looked to me more like hunger.

The preacher was waiting, I think, till everybody was focused directly on him. Then, without warning, he suddenly turned and pounded his fist on the table, which set up a strange racket from the boxes. I must have been the only one surprised, because no one else jumped at the noise. I gave a little hiccupy shudder that threatened to turn into full-blown shakes.

Stepmama's hand reached out for mine. Not to comfort, but to silence me.

"Be silent, child," she hissed, "and be ready to learn."

I turned to her. "Learn what?"

She smiled and I bent my head under that uncomfort-

· · · · · · · ·

able grimace. Her voice came hissing again toward me. "The Craft," she said.

"What craft? Knitting? Needlework?" *And why*, I thought, *would I learn it here in this strange church?*

She snatched her hand from mine. "Stupid girl. The Craft that shapes the world."

I couldn't think what she meant and shook my head.

"It starts here. Open yourself to it."

I couldn't speak but shook my head again.

"Stupid. Child." Then she leaned forward and watched, totally transfixed, as the preacher took a little hop-step toward us holding his Bible in one hand; his face was full of a kind of happiness and yet sad, too.

The preacher stared at the congregation, saying, "There is death in those boxes. But life as well. As it was promised to us. If we believe. If we are strong enough to believe." He opened the Bible and thrust his finger down at a passage. "Mark chapter 16, verses 16 to 18," he said.

Mark chapter 16, verses 16 to 18. I sure wished I knew what those verses were about.

A soft rattle of *amens* sounded all around me. I said *amen*, too. Just in case.

A woman behind me began crying out, "Lord, God . . ." And then what followed was a long line of nonsense words,

· · · · · · · ·

or foreign words, sounding like "La-la-lal-bam-balling-ing-star-randle" and so forth. Gibberish. I started to turn around to look at her, but Stepmama grabbed me by the arm and pulled me back.

Another woman, small, wiry, came forward with a tray on which sat three glasses and a pitcher in which a tiny bit of clear liquid sloshed. She put it to the side of the boxes, then nodded at the preacher.

"And death as well as life . . . " the preacher continued, "in the drink."

"Strychnine," whispered Stepmama, leaning forward eagerly.

It wasn't just plain water in that pitcher. I knew how poisonous strychnine was—Papa used it to get rid of mice where he stored the seeds. I started to stand up, thinking that there was little that was holy in *this* church, but Stepmama gripped my arm and pulled me down and closer to her.

"Mark chapter 16, verses 16 to 18," cried a man's voice somewhere in the room.

The preacher nodded. "Amen, brother."

The trickle of *amen*s around the room opened up again until it was a flood. This time I wasn't carried on the wave of emotion but began whispering *amen* over and over out of fear, until it began to sound just like the other woman's gibberish.

. . . .

At that, Stepmama let go of my arm, misreading my response, and I let her think I was under the church's spell. If that let me get away from With Signs, I'd babble away all night.

The preacher raised his hand to quiet everyone and then, in a small, almost secretive voice, he whispered, "Where there is the Believer, there, too, is the Way."

This time when he turned to the table, he slapped the Bible down on it, and the strange buzzing noise started again.

There was *something* in those boxes, but I didn't know what.

"Let us sing," the preacher said. And we began a rousing chorus of "We Shall Not Be Moved," which drowned out all other sounds.

While we were singing, the two helpers got up, went over to the stove. One came back with a jar of what turned out to be kerosene because when the other stuck a burning brand from the stove into it, flames flared up.

I wondered what the jar was for but didn't have to wait long for an answer. When they got back to the preacher with the burning jar, he reached out for it and held it under his chin with the flames still flaring up. His lips darkened till it looked as if he'd been eating ashes. The sight made me shudder again, tremors rippling across my shoulders, partly with horror and fear, partly with wonder and awe.

· · · · · · · ·

The congregation started out singing again, "Wheel in a Wheel," and the room almost burst with the song. I found myself singing along. Stepmama didn't sing, of course, but she nodded in time as if satisfied with me joining in.

The preacher licked his blackened lips and gave the jar back to the dark-haired man. Only then did horror and fear win out, and I felt my stomach turning sour as if I'd eaten something rotten. I wondered if I was going to throw up and fought it down. But a kind of shadow of that sour taste remained in my mouth.

"Stepmama," I said, turning to her, wanting to ask where the toilet was or if this place only had an outhouse. More than that, I had to get away from the church, where boxes buzzed, people screamed out in gibberish, there was strychnine in a pitcher, and a preacher held burning kerosene under his chin till his lips turned black. I wanted to be back in Cousin Nancy's church, where Jesus—heart in hand—looked down on me with his comforting gaze.

"Be quiet," Stepmama snapped, but continued to stare at the preacher, her lips curved up in a semblance of a smile.

I tried to quiet my stomach, my heart, my fear. I was not entirely successful.

The woman behind me started up again, shouting out her nonsense, and then I heard her stand up. When she

. . . .

walked past me to the front, I saw it was the pregnant girl. Her arms were up in the air and she had her head thrown back. All the while she kept on gabbling, "Noo-na-nannno-sing-a-bam-Lord Jesus-mam-a-bobble," babbling over and over. And then she flung herself down onto the floor onto her side and then her back—it would have been hard to go forward onto her stomach for she was *that* pregnant. Her legs and arms began to flail about. But she never missed a beat.

At last her gabbling sank to a murmur. The two helpers on either side of the preacher came over to get her up, propping her into a sitting position till her voice trailed off in silence. Then they eased her onto her feet and steered her back to her seat while all around the *amen*s came fast and furious, though this time I resisted joining them.

I couldn't understand why Stepmama had brought me to this place and just as I was about to say something to her, the preacher started speaking again. His voice was at first like a dry rustle but it soon gained in power and intensity. I turned back, drawn in by his words.

"I've *seen* the spirit of the Lord," he whispered. And then, louder, "Spirit. Of. The. Lord." He rocked back and forth on the last four words.

"Amen!" called out the pregnant woman.

. . . .

"It follows me like a cloud overhead," said the preacher. "But not a thundercloud, oh no. This cloud is long and blue and electric. The color of God's true love for us."

"Let it shine, brother," someone called out, and the congregation answered with the hymn "This Little Light of Mine," which I know and so I sang along for a while, just to calm myself more than anything else. But soon half the congregation was up and dancing in front of the table, arms in the air swaying, including the pregnant girl.

I thought about getting up and dancing my way around the room, then making a break for the door. But it was dark, there was a long road home, and Stepmama was sure to catch up with me. Her punishment would be . . . Well, I couldn't guess what it would be. But something awful, I was sure.

Just then, the pregnant girl started to flail about again and sink to her knees, but this time someone caught her, a man—maybe her husband—who held her in his arms and they swayed together until the hymn was done and he walked her carefully back to her seat and the dancing was over and so was my chance to get away.

The whole thing seemed like playacting somehow. We'd done plays in school, but none as strange as this, and I was having trouble getting my mind around it. I couldn't laugh

· · · · · · · ·

though it had some funny moments, because underneath there was a deep strangeness that was truly scary.

As it turned out, the strangeness still had a ways to go, for when everyone who'd been dancing sat down again, the preacher walked back to the table and moved one of the wooden boxes forward.

"The devil comes in the night," he declared, now in full throat. No more whispers. "The devil *riiiiiiides* the south wind." He strung out the word *ride* until it was like he was singing it. "The hot wind. The wind from Hell."

"It's been blowing, brother!" shouted the blond-haired helper.

"And we know . . . " said the preacher, stepping forward and then back, rocking as he spoke, "we *KNOW* what that means."

"Tell us, oh, tell us!" someone from the back cried out.

Stepmama moved a bit, shifting her weight forward, leaning toward the preacher again, her mouth unaccountably open as if to receive some kind of communion.

"Who's ready to go?" the preacher continued. "Who's ready to do what the apostle tells us to do? Shall we? Shall we *alllllll* do it? Shall we take up our deaths? Show the Lord we're not afraid because we live forever in His holy name? Shall we . . . ?" He stepped forward till he was

. . . .

standing over Stepmama and me, sweating now as he had not been sweating when the fire had been held beneath his chin. I saw a drop roll down his forehead and slide down his cheek, resting on the point of his long chin. I was hypnotized by that drop. I couldn't stop staring at it.

Then Stepmama slipped a white handkerchief out of her pocketbook and handed it up to the preacher, who took it without a word, wiped his face, then handed it back to her and she spread the handkerchief on her lap. Neither one of them looked directly at the other the entire time, and it felt like a long-practiced move.

Turning back to the table, the preacher put his hand atop one of the boxes. The strange rustling sound commenced again. "If we *belieeeeeve* in the Lord, if we follow his wishes, we will not be taken this night," he said. "Not you, brothers. Not you, sisters. Not any of us. Because we believe."

Stepmama sat back on the bench, as if satisfied. She crossed her right ankle over her left, her hands down by her sides. The white handkerchief, damp with the preacher's sweat, was still spread out across her lap.

"Do it, brother," a man called out. "Do it now, Brother. We're with you. Let the Lord see how much you believe."

The pregnant girl started babbling again.

The preacher took the top off the box and pulled out something long and thick and dark. And when it started

· · · · · · · ·

to twine itself round and about his hand, I realized it was a rattlesnake. The preacher moved toward the congregation again with his now-familiar rocking step. "And these signs," he said, "shall follow them that believe."

He turned to the left. "In my name they shall cast out devils. Yes, they shall!" He turned to the right. "They shall speak with new tongues. Yes, they shall!" He stood dead center and held the snake above his head with one hand. "They shall take up serpents. And if they drink any deadly thing, it shall not hurt them. That's in Mark, verses 16 to 18."

With his free hand he gestured toward the pitcher and the glasses, which up till that moment I'd forgotten all about. After that he began inching closer and closer to the front benches, the snake now cradled in his arms.

Where we sat.

Stepmama and me.

Caressing the snake's spade-like head, the preacher suddenly leaned over and kissed the top of it.

The snake paid him no attention but looked straight at me, its smile startlingly familiar. It took me a moment before I realized it was exactly Stepmama's smile.

Then the rattler opened its mouth. That mouth was dark, cavernous, the teeth shiny. Its forked tongue flicked out. At me.

. . . .

That was when I felt myself slipping sidewise into the darkness, down and down and down right onto Stepmama's lap, with the left side of my head on the damp white handkerchief.

I don't recall being carried to the car or anything about the drive home. I don't remember getting sick. When we arrived back in Addison, Stepmama left me there in the car, its windows all opened wide, to wake up on my own, my dress spoiled and smelling of vomit.

It was early Monday morning when I woke at last, the sun not yet over Elk Mountain, so the sky had that pearly look. My mouth felt full of cotton. My stomach ached. I was shaking with the cold. And the smell in the car was unbelievable.

I gathered myself together slowly, managed to get out of the car, and hobbled to the house on wobbly legs. At least Stepmama had left the front door unlocked. For such small favors I had to be grateful.

As I walked into the house, my left hand on the wall to keep from falling, I remembered some of what had happened at the church as if it was a series of small black-and-white photographs: the handsome blond boy looking at me, the preacher speaking about Mark 16 to 18, the pregnant girl

. . . .

reciting gibberish, the wild singing and clapping that had set up echoes in my heart, the burning kerosene in the jar turning the preacher's lips black, the poison in the pitcher. I could scarcely make sense of it. Images tumbled about in my head like water over stones.

Water over stones.

Papa used to say water had to travel over twenty-one stones to be pure. I shook my head. I didn't believe there was *anything* pure going on in that church last night, and I trembled with the memories.

But once I'd washed my face, brushed my teeth, changed out of my stinking clothes, and fallen into bed, it was the snake I dreamed about.

Only the snake.

·19·

AN UNWANTED VISITOR

stayed home from school Monday because my legs were still trembling and my stomach threatened to empty again. I had what Stepmama called the cramps and she was—all unaccountably—nice to me. She brought me warm milk and buttered toast, leaving it outside my door for she still could not come in because of the rowan branch. She even dropped off a note at school

saying as how I was going to take a few days off to recover from a "visitor" though there was no one visiting us at all.

When I protested the lie, she laughed without humor. "That's what we call it in Charleston," she said. "Your teacher will understand."

But I didn't. Not until later did I find out that "the visitor" was what more sophisticated girls called the monthlies. That and saying they'd "fallen off the roof." And "Aunt Flo's come to stay." And even "on the rag."

I felt listless and crampy, so I napped a lot and read—reread, really—all of the fairy tales in my books as well as *A Girl of the Limberlost* and *Anne of Green Gables*. I looked out the window of my bedroom at the sunny days going by. I did my homework, which Stepmama brought back from school for me.

All in all, I stayed away from school two days. The cramping came and went, as did the blood. The first day it was spotty, the next day not there at all.

Stepmama waited on me, which should have made me suspicious, but only gave me hope that the worst with her was finally over. Maybe she'd just needed that much time till she realized she loved me. Then Papa would get better and we'd be a real family instead of—what we were.

· · · · · · · ·

Of course, that kind of hope is just a parcel of magic thoughts without the actual magic to make anything happen.

By the third day, I went to school because at home it had begun to feel as if I'd been imprisoned. No bars on the door, but shut in nonetheless. Stepmama's concerns now seemed as if the show was more important than her actually being there. What hope I had was gone. Somehow that made me even sadder than before.

Will it be this way each month? I wondered. *Will she keep me in my room every thirty days, not by the force of her will but by my acquiescence? Acquiescence* was a word I'd just learned in civics class. It means how a person acts when she knowingly and without protest lets someone else take her rights away. And that's what I was doing with Stepmama. Letting her tell me what to do and say and believe, without saying a word against her power.

I excused myself because I was only twelve. Because I worried about Papa. Because I wanted a real mama. Because I was, somehow, all alone. But those were only excuses. I acquiesced, plain and simple.

No—I promised myself. *If I am truly becoming a woman by this pain, I should act like one.*

. . . .

So, I got out of my nightgown, dressed, and went into the living room, where Papa drowsed in his everlasting dream. I was ready to tell Stepmama I was fine and wanted to go back to school. I would demand to go back. As for With Signs church, I would never, ever go there again.

But Stepmama was nowhere around.

I tapped lightly on her bedroom door, in case she was napping. When there was no answer, I peered out the window. The car was gone. She was gone. For a moment my heart lifted. But I knew she'd be gone only for as long as her chores took.

I went back to her room and carefully turned the handle of the door. It opened with nary a sound. The room was completely dark; the heavy curtains covering the two windows let in no light.

"Stepmama," I said, "I'm feeling much better." Then I asked, "Are you here?" Just in case.

A voice whispered out of the darkness, "Is that a true question for me, Snow in Summer?"

It wasn't Stepmama's voice, but it was a voice I knew though I'd heard it only once long before. Heard and tried to forget. But magic is hard to forget.

I slipped into the darkened room. "Mirror," I said, "not that question, but another one."

· · · · · · · ·

153

"Speak it then," the mirror told me.

I'd had a question that had been tangling my brain ever since Stepmama had come to live with us. Till now, I hadn't had a chance nor the courage nor the incentive to enter Stepmama's room again to ask it.

"Mirror . . ." I hesitated, took a deep breath, got my courage up, and asked: "Who should I fear the most?"

I'd always thought that the answer was going to be that I had to fear Stepmama the most, so I hadn't wanted to waste the question. But after seeing the snake in the preacher's hands, I was no longer so sure which was worse—the witch or the serpent.

In the dark, something stirred. There was a shussshing sound. I shuddered. Did Stepmama keep snakes here? Even if they were in boxes, the sound was enough to make my knees go weak. If there were serpents in the house, as well as Stepmama, then both my greatest fears were realized together.

Suddenly the mirror turned on, lit up like a picture show. Years ago, when she was nearly ready to give birth to my brother, Mama had taken me to a picture show. It was called *Mickey's Garden*. I remembered bits of it now: inchworms grown as big as snakes, trying to eat both Mickey and his dog.

• • • • • • • •

"Fear the Hunter," the mirror's masked face said, startling me out of my memories.

"Fear the Hunter, fear the knife,
Fear the edge that takes a life."

The mirror spoke as if *Hunter* was capitalized, like a name or a rank of some kind.

"The Hunter? Who's that?" I asked, but the mirror had gone silent. In the silence I heard a car door slam right outside.

Stepmama was home.

I slipped back out of her room so fast my shadow had trouble keeping up, and I headed down the hallway as if going toward the bathroom.

That was where she found me. "Up on your feet at last," she said, almost sneeringly.

"I'm feeling much better." It wasn't a lie.

"Good, because I've got a little surprise for you." She smiled one of her discomforting smiles, then turned away and went into the kitchen. Watching her back—so straight, so confident—I shuddered. But the mirror had not said to fear her. Or the snake. It had said to fear the Hunter. So I relaxed my guard.

. . . .

I did wonder about that surprise she'd promised, but I wondered even more who that hunter might turn out to be. Then I thought that the mirror might actually have meant Stepmama was the hunter but didn't dare name her. Certainly she hunted a willing partner. Or even an unwilling one. Or maybe the mirror meant the snake was the hunter? Its mouth surely hunted an exposed arm or leg or neck. Or perhaps the mirror meant I should fear the preacher, who'd clearly been hunting for my immortal soul. That's the trouble with mirror answers. You can see more than one meaning in them.

At that, I laughed nervously. *Foolish Summer. If you have to rely on answers from a mirror to guide you, you're already lost.*

I promised myself never to ask the mirror my third question. Not even if my life depended upon it.

I went off to school the next day and so had three full days to think about the hunter. But think as long and as hard as I might, no further explanations came to me.

I even looked up *the Hunter* in our classroom encyclopedia. The only listing was for *Orion* under *Greek mythology.* He owned two dogs and hunted lions. As far as I knew, there were no lions in West Virginia. Unless you

· · · · · · · ·

counted *painters,* which is what people call mountain lions, though there are hardly any of those left in our county.

My teacher asked if I was feeling better, and I said, "Never better," though that wasn't entirely true. However, it was fear that troubled me now. My first monthly was over and gone.

And good riddance, I thought.

Saturday morning I woke up early. Tomorrow would be Sunday, and with it churchgoing.

I wrestled with how to get out of being hauled back to the snake church. I knew Stepmama was sure to insist on it, which left me but a day and a night to figure out how to escape.

Cousin Nancy had told me once that making a list of my *do's* and *don'ts* and *maybes* could help me make decisions. Though this was more of a *wills* and *won'ts.*

So I tried it, but just in my head. I didn't want Stepmama to get hold of any written list and task me with it.

Wills: Keep Stepmama sweet. Ask to go to Cousin Nancy's church.

Won'ts: SNAKES!!!! Poison. Burning glasses. Crazy folk.

It was what I knew already. It was no help at all.

· · · · · · · ·

I could try and run away, but except for Cousin Nancy's house, I'd nowhere to run. And Cousin Nancy's would be the very first place Stepmama would look for me. If she wanted to find me, that is. I knew by now that she didn't particularly like me. Maybe even hated me. I'd never understood why. I tried hard to make her love me, did all the chores she set me to, did well in school. And it was clear she wanted me for something, though maybe just to do the washing and the gardening or to keep Papa calm and sweet.

Papa! I'd almost forgotten Papa in all my fears. If I ran off, what would happen to him?

It was a puzzle. I'd never liked puzzles. I liked stories, ones that ended happily ever after. And I sure couldn't wrap my mind about a happy ending to this one.

I planned and plotted all through the morning and came up with nothing. And in the afternoon, as she said she would, Stepmama surprised me.

The choices I made after that had as much to do with fear as love, more to do with the moment than any kind of a plan.

Stepmama knocked on my door and said in a voice that was happier than I'd ever heard from her that after I was done with any homework and chores, we were going visiting.

. . . .

Going visiting—that was something we'd never done before.

"Oh—and wear that pretty blue dress." She stood in the doorway and smiled at me. A plain, honest-to-goodness smile that even touched her eyes.

I dared to hope we'd be going to Cousin Nancy's. With Stepmama in this new, almost giddy mood, perhaps we could all be friends. It worked in stories, like *Anne of Green Gables*. *Maybe*, I thought, *maybe I wasn't trying hard enough before.*

"Yes, Stepmama," I said, grinning back at her. "There's not much left to do."

The last of my chores was hanging out Stepmama's washing on the line. It was a soft spring day, the sun bright overhead, and the wash would be dry by the time we got back from wherever the visit would be. I'd even offer to do the ironing for her. Normally ironing was the one thing she liked to do on her own.

My homework being long finished, I got dressed as she asked, in the blue dress that Cousin Nancy and her church ladies had gotten me out of the free box down in the town center. Cousin Nancy had sewn some old lace for a collar, which totally transformed the dress, and Miss Caroline and Miss Amelia had contributed a blue ribbon from

· · · · · · · ·

their trousseau chests to go as a belt for my waist. I let my hair out of its braids and brushed it out, fifty strokes. It lay on my shoulders in soft waves.

Stepmama took me into her room on her own accord, tied a kerchief around my neck, wrong way around, like a movie cowboy I'd seen on a poster outside of the picture show. Then she dusted my cheeks and chin with some powder that made me sneeze and ran a bit of color over my lips. Not red like hers but a soft rose.

Taking away the kerchief, she held out a hand mirror so I could see myself. I looked like someone else, not me. Someone older. Someone sophisticated. Someone pretty.

"Better," she said. "Like a Charleston girl." She nodded.

Though inside I still felt like me.

I thought about being Anne Shirley at Green Gables, a bit prickly at first but later learning to speak sympathetically, and managed to say, "Thank you, Stepmama." My voice was suddenly different as I said the words: lower, sweeter, friendlier.

"*Much* better," she answered, and off we went. In the car. Not to Cousin Nancy's, then, but quickly out of town and up the mountain again.

At that, my stomach clenched. My hands wrangled in my lap. She hadn't said *where* we were going. But it wasn't

· · · · · · · ·

a Sunday. We were too dressed up. She had on her bright red lipstick and her nails were freshly painted.

But With Signs might have services on Saturdays, too. Some churches did. Maybe at their Saturday services people dressed properly.

Maybe it all depended on the snakes' handlers.

And the snakes.

I stared out of the car window as the trees whizzed by, bands of green and gold. I was much too afraid to ask where we were going. Too afraid I already knew. I couldn't leap out with the car speeding along. So I said nothing, not in my new friendly voice nor in my old scared one. But my stomach hurt so much, it was like I was getting the monthlies all over again.

. . . .

·20·

COUSIN NANCY REMEMBERS

hat Saturday was a day I'll always remember. I'd just closed the post office and was pulling down the shades when that witch drove by going hell-bent. Normally I wouldn't have cared, but she had Summer with her and they were heading out of town.

Curious, I thought. Except for last week when she'd taken Summer off to church, I didn't remember that child

· · · · · · · ·

having a ride in her stepmama's precious Chevrolet in a coon's age. Not even when it was raining or snowing and Summer had to slog her way up the hill to go to school and back down again to go home, poor mite.

The car was a dark green, like sludge in water near a coal mine, and I've never liked that color or make of car since.

I wouldn't have thought any more of it, excepting Summer didn't drive back with her when she returned. I saw that plain as plain. And when had that woman ever left Summer off with friend or foe excepting me, and even then she did it begrudgingly.

In fact, it turned out Summer didn't come home that night or the next—her teacher told me some story about her taking sick and not being to school for a full week, but she hadn't looked sick in the car. And she wasn't at home being cared for. I knew because the next day after church, I went by the house when Summer's stepmama was out, peered in the windows since I still refused to go inside. Besides, it wouldn't have been polite. And the door was locked tight. From the outside.

Except for seeing the top of Lem's head as he dozed in his chair, I couldn't spot a soul in the house. I looked in every single window. I reported this to the police. It took them days to believe me, over another week to check it out.

· · · · · · · ·

Not that I'd ever pestered the police before. But the chief took me for an addled widow of a certain age. Mind you, I'm barely twenty-nine. Well, thirty-three on a bad day.

"She's my *goddaughter*," I said in exasperation. "She's not thirteen yet. Not for another two months."

It didn't help that I called her stepmama a witch. Or that the chief, Charlie Hatfield, who'd been in my class in school and was a fat little oinker then as now, said, "Nan, everybody knows you've always been sweet on Lem . . ."

As if that mattered at all when a child is missing.

Then he smiled conspiratorially at me, which made his cheeks plump up even more and his eyes squint so tight, they became like slits. He looked right ready for the slop bucket, did Charlie. "Some girls run off to be with a boy when they're thirteen," he said, "and there ain't a law in our whole state says we have to try and get her back."

"She doesn't *know* any boys," I told him.

"Of course she does," he retorted, ending the conversation.

·21·

HUNTER

e went up the mountain, rounding that same scary hairpin turn going out of town. If anything, the trees overhead seemed to bend over us even more than the last time. I felt sick to my stomach with fear and the car's sliding about the curves of the road. I opened my window, hoping to suck in some calming air. It wouldn't have done me any good to beg Stepmama to slow down. It might have even encouraged her to go faster.

· · · · · · ·

"Close your window," Stepmama said, keeping her eyes on the curving road and not even looking in my direction from the corner of her eye.

For once I disobeyed her.

I guessed that convinced her that if I didn't keep the window down, I might throw up in her car again. She didn't say a word more.

If I thought that was a victory, I was mistaken. But then I was always mistaken when it came to Stepmama.

We drove for maybe a half hour more before she abruptly turned off onto a country lane. It wasn't the lane I was expecting, the one that led to the With Signs church. Instead it was a narrower, longer drive, lined with birch trees that were so tightly planted and so large, they made an archway and almost seemed to glow in the dark made by their own leaves.

I let out the breath I hadn't known I was holding. My stomach suddenly relaxed. No snakes, then.

Ahead was a shabby yellow trailer parked in the exact center of the clearing in the middle of a stand of pines. To the right was a small, badly tended garden going to weed and seed. I couldn't see a thing in it that wasn't too small, too hard, or rotten.

Nailed to one of the pine trees to the left of the house was a target. There were three filthy arrows sticking in the bull's-eye.

· · · · · · · ·

Stepmama slowed, then stopped the car and only then said, "Roll up your window and get out."

This time I obeyed her.

The minute we were out of the car, the door of the trailer opened and someone came out and stood on the concrete step, hands on his hips. Blond, heavy-lidded, he was as blandly handsome as one of the princes in the pictures of my fairy-tale book, though not wearing armor but more conventionally dressed in tan slacks and a striped shirt, the sleeves rolled up. His hair was slicked back. He rolled a toothpick in his mouth and smiled around it.

And then I knew him. He was the older boy from the With Signs church, the one who'd nodded at Stepmama. The one who'd looked so satisfied with himself. He was still looking satisfied, though why anyone who lived in such a run-down trailer with such an unkempt garden should feel that way escaped me.

Stepmama shepherded me toward him, and when we were close enough, she said, "Hunter, this is Snow."

Hunter.

I went cold all over. Surely this was the one the mirror had warned me about. *But why?* He hadn't any knife on him that I could see. And he didn't look fierce, only fatuous, and that's a word that means "silly in a self-satisfied way."

· · · · · · · ·

167

"Yes, ma'am," he said, and spit out the toothpick, ran his hand back across his hair, and came down off the step, as eager as a pup in training.

He reached out to shake my hand, and his hand was large enough to entirely envelop mine.

I looked over at Stepmama and she crooked her finger at me.

I began to tremble, I'd no idea why, and tried to pull my hand away, but Hunter held it tight.

As he looked down at me, his big blue eyes seemed somehow comforting. The smile wasn't so much fatuous as hopeful. A bit of wind from the east tousled his hair and pushed it across his broad forehead, softening how he looked.

"Hello, Snow," he said. "We gonna be friends?" His voice had that soft lilt that some of the local boys have, but with a strange twang, too, as if he'd been studying from the radio or picture shows how to speak to girls.

I tried to smile back and couldn't quite manage it, frozen as I was. But suddenly I felt my cheeks get hot and knew I was blushing in a way I'd never blushed before.

"When Hunter saw you last week in church, he asked me if you and he could walk out together," Stepmama said. "And I told him you were just barely become a woman, but I would introduce you to him and see what happens."

· · · · · · · ·

I could have asked why he should have said any such thing. After all, I didn't think of myself as a great beauty. Or asked when he'd had time to ask her. Surely not after I'd passed out in church and then thrown up. Surely not then.

But I stopped wondering about that almost at once. And I conveniently forgot the mirror's warning, forgot that I'd only just met Hunter, that Stepmama had made this promise without consulting me, that he must be five years older than me. Or more.

"Hello, Hunter," I said softly, my voice nowhere near as loud as my beating heart. And at that very moment, I also inconveniently forgot to be afraid.

We stood in an attitude of talking, my right hand in his, but said nothing at all. I no longer needed his strength to keep my hand in his. It nestled there all by itself. And while we stood that way, hand in hand, my face got hotter, but his smile never changed. Still we couldn't manage a word between us.

In the middle of all that stillness, I heard a sudden strange click. And then another, and then the roar of Stepmama's engine. Before I could turn my head to see, she'd peeled out of Hunter's driveway and left me to my fate.

My fate. All I could think of was that if I was deep into first love, it wasn't sweet at all like the songs on the radio

. . . .

said, nor the stories in my books. It was like a knife in my heart. Perhaps that was what the mirror had meant.

Surprisingly, such an idea was both exciting and terrifying, painful and pleasant all at the same time.

Once the sound of Stepmama's car was out of our hearing, Hunter cleared his throat. "Do you wanna come inside?" he said, his hand still clutching mine.

"Inside where?"

"Inside the house." He looked at me as if I was stupid.

I thought for a moment, because suddenly—almost as if someone was whispering to me—I heard "Too quick. Too quick." I shook my head.

"Can we . . . can we walk a bit? And talk?" I asked. I needed the air right now, to cool my blazing cheeks, so I could breathe.

He looked down at me. "Talk? What do you wanna talk about?"

About why you asked Stepmama if we could court, I thought, but didn't say it aloud. I shrugged. "You could tell me something about you. All I know is your name."

He smiled again, that melting smile. Then he shrugged back. "You can see me," he said. "Not much to tell. I'm twenty-three and single. And you're—what—sixteen or so. And single, too." His hand was suddenly hot and moist.

. . . .

"Not thirteen yet," I said.

Something like a startled frown crossed his face, but briefly. "You're mighty sophisticated for thirteen." Only he said *sir-fister-cated.*

"Not quite thirteen," I repeated.

"Whatever."

I swallowed hard, tried again. Behind us there were birds calling. A crow, I thought. Several crows. I suddenly remembered that a group of crows was called a *murder.*

But Hunter was smiling again and my knees went weak. I struggled to say something different, something original, something fetching, before coming up with, "Tell me about With Signs church. Why do you go there?" And immediately afterward I was embarrassed to have said it.

He let my hand go and then wiped his own hand on the side of his slacks. His hand had been sweating, or mine had, or both of ours had. But it felt somehow as if he was trying to wipe me off. He thought for a long time before speaking.

"I like the snakes," he said at last. "And the girls who like snakes."

"I . . . I don't like snakes." My voice had gotten so hushed he had to lean in to watch my lips.

"Oh, that'll come. When you believe."

· · · · · · · ·

I wasn't sure I could wrap myself in that particular cloak, but didn't say so. I wanted him to keep liking me, snakes or not.

"So—now you wanna come into the house? I got ice cream. And beer."

I didn't really want ice cream. My stomach was tumbling over and over, doing handstands, backflips, somersaults. And of course I'd never had beer. I was too young for it. "I don't think so. Can't we just walk a bit?" My hand, the one that bore the imprint of his, made a kind of waving motion toward the path.

"I guess . . . ," he said, but didn't manage to make it sound as if he thought it was a good idea. Reaching into his pocket, he pulled out another toothpick, stuck it in his mouth, turned on his heel, and started to walk off into the woods ahead of me, moving so swiftly, I had to double-time to catch up to him.

It seemed an odd beginning to what was supposed to be a courtship. But as I'd had only the fairy stories and *Anne of Green Gables* to go by, I supposed it was going all right. After all, look at what Cinderella and Sleeping Beauty had to go through before they won their princes. And Anne and Gilbert managed to fall in love by being rivals first. So perhaps this was how true love was supposed to go in real life. Though deep inside, something was nagging at me.

· · · · · · · ·

We walked in silence into the woods, not the comfortable kind of silence I had with Cousin Nancy or the edgy, angry silences between Stepmama and me or the tragic silences that had become my only communication with Papa. This was a silence compounded of stranger-ness, where two people with absolutely nothing in common can't think of a thing to say.

So I began to babble to fill the empty spaces. As we walked, I jabbered away at the things I knew: plants that Papa had shown me. Or wildflowers that Mama had loved. Or the wild herbs that Cousin Nancy knew. I pointed out a cluster of bloodroot, on the forest floor, with its scalloped leaves and white, daisy-like flowers. "I like the little white flowers and the yellow centers, don't you?" And then I added, "Did you know, there's a reddish juice in the stems and roots. *She-roots*, Papa calls them. You can grind the dried roots into a powder to be used for . . ." My voice trailed off.

"Yes," he said. Or at least it was a grunt that sounded like *yes*.

We passed some yellow-belled flowers and I knelt down, trying to be as graceful as a princess. "Trout lilies, Papa calls these." I didn't tell him Papa hadn't called things much of anything lately, not since Stepmama came. After all, Hunter and I weren't yet close enough for that kind of

· · · · · · · ·

confession. "Papa says it's because they look like the coloring on a brook trout."

"Not *much* like," Hunter growled.

We walked about a dozen more steps in silence, but when we passed by a stand of high grass where some busy spider had spun a web between two stalks, I said, "Did you know that spiderwebs can be used to stop someone bleeding, and—"

"Can it stop you talking?" He was no longer smiling that slow smile, and his lips had thinned down to a gash. For the first time, I saw something mean in his narrowing eyes. He was still chewing on that toothpick until he suddenly spit it out as if it—or something else—had left a bad taste in his mouth.

"Hunter?" My voice squeaked a little. It was as if we'd both suddenly fallen out of whatever spell had been placed upon us.

He bit his lip, realizing he was scaring me, and I saw him trying to rearrange his features so he could be attractive again. For a moment he looked like a little boy who'd had a scolding and knew he had to seem innocent and sorry at the same time. Running his fingers through his hair, he leaned toward me as if to tell me a secret. "So, Snow, you ready to go back to the house now?"

· · · · · · · ·

"I prefer to be called Summer."

"So, *Summer,*" his voice suddenly soft, low, as if softness would be more enticing, though in fact it made him all the scarier. "We go back to the house and you can have some ice cream, I can have that beer." He smiled slowly, once again sure of his charm. There was a practiced element in his wooing, learned but not felt. As if someone had told him how to do it. "I got vanilla *and* chocolate." This time the smile actually reached his eyes.

I wondered if the smile might have more to do with the possibility of that beer.

"No, thank you," I said.

"Look, we're going to the house." He was trying hard to hold on to his charm and failing. There was an edge to his voice.

"Trailer," I said, not trying to be charming at all.

"Now, Summer, we can do this the easy way," he said flatly, "or the hard way." There was the smile again and now it seemed only sinister. *Sinister*—a word I'd read in stories but never heard said out loud, but the perfect word for how he looked. I was thinking about that as he finished his thought.

"I prefer this the easy way, though your mama—"

"Stepmama . . . " I said automatically.

. . . .

A small wind began puzzling through the trees. Something white floated off to the side of my seeing. I suddenly remembered a song of Papa's about a little girl sleeping in the pines where the sun never shines and shivering the whole night through.

"I believe your stepmama prefers the hard way. Though she also wants it done far from home. Now *there*'s a woman loves snakes."

"Stepmama *is* a snake!" I was surprised I'd said it aloud, surprised at the fierceness in my voice.

"Why," he drawled, "I believe she is. Maybe *that*'s what I love about her." That's when he grinned mightily and bent down.

I watched as if mesmerized as he lifted his pants leg to reach into a sheath tied to his calf, a sheath where he'd hidden his knife. When he stood up again, knife in hand, I was already running as hard as I could down the long driveway.

About halfway, I looked once over my shoulder to gauge the distance between us and saw with astonishment that Hunter was down on his knees, hands over his face to shield it from the razor-sharp talons of a white owl that was beating its wings against his head.

I didn't know owls did that. Not in the daylight. Not to human beings. But I whispered a prayer as I ran: "Thank

. . . .

you, God," and wondered if I'd been saved by an angel, not an owl.

I knew I couldn't count on Hunter being held off for long. And so I kept running as fast as possible, not down the driveway, where Hunter surely would have caught me, but instead plunging off to the left, into the darkening woods.

·22·

STEPMAMA REMEMBERS

drove off and felt free—free at last—of that burdensome child. I'd tried my best with sweetness and with pain to bring her to the Craft. But you cannot make someone do what they will not do and expect them to thank you for it. Master knew that. Told me so often. I was the first and only apprentice he'd ever kept. The rest he sucked dry of their seven years and threw them out. But I had *wanted* what he had to give, wanted

it passionately, and the years I gratefully gave him were the best ones he'd ever had.

Snow was no such creature. She had to be gotten rid of. I do believe if I'd tried to take her years, they'd have poisoned me.

My plan in place, I knew I'd a few weeks' grace before she'd be missed. A few weeks to take her fading father to the hospital to die and to play the grieving widow. A few weeks till I could collect my widow's pension. And a few weeks after that to sell off the land to the railroad bosses and go sorrowfully back to Charleston to start my life anew.

Charleston? Why, with the money I'd be getting, I could go to Ohio. Or even California, where the hankering after magic is mighty strong. It made me smile to think of all those movie folk, untouched by the recessions, ready for fleecing.

I made it back to Lemuel's house—I'd never thought of it as mine—and there took a long bath with candles set out all around, the water freshened with rose petals and lavender from the garden.

Free.

Free!

The next morning, as I was brushing my hair a hundred strokes, I twitched the drape off the mirror.

· · · · · · · ·

The mirror's dark mask of a face swam into view.

"Mistress," it said.

Never Master, I thought, grinding my teeth in frustration.

"What is your question?"

"No question at all," I told the thing. "Just wanted to let you know that the girl Snow is gone. Finished. Her heart cut out and stewed. Bones scattered. What do you think of that?"

The mask turned, became sharper, the edges of the black more defined. Then it said,

> *"Oh, Mistress, that she's lost is true,*
> *But still she'll have the best of you."*

"Best of *me,* you stupid mirror, no one has ever gotten the best of me. Not the Master, not lovesick Lemuel, not that puling Nancy, and certainly not the girl. She's dead and gone by now. I've made sure of it. Besides, I didn't even ask a question of you."

I threw the brush at the mirror as hard as I could. Even as it hit and shattered a corner of the glass, I realized that in fact I *had* asked. And the mirror had answered.

Only the answer made no sense at all.

· · · · · · · ·

·23·

NIGHT ON ELK MOUNTAIN

'd no hope of simply outrunning Hunter. He was bigger than me, had longer legs than me, knew these woods better than I did. Heck, I didn't know them at all.

All I had was fear, which is a great motivator. And I was small, so I could hide. I had to make use of the present of time that the white owl's intervention had given me, the present of a good head start.

. . . .

Lucky for me I was wearing a dark-colored dress, not pink or yellow, either of which would have shone like a beacon against the green and brown of the woods.

"Thank you, Stepmama," I whispered, and really meant it this time because it had been Stepmama who'd insisted I wear the blue dress. Possibly she thought because it made me look quite a bit older. But whatever her reason, it might just save my life.

Then I heard Hunter behind me, calling out.

"Snow," he shouted, "come back. It was a joke."

Summer, I thought. *No joke.*

I kept on running.

And then a little later, a bit farther away, as if he'd gone looking for me down the rest of the driveway, out onto the road, "Snow, damn you, come back."

But Snow wasn't my name and I wouldn't answer to it.

I headed *up* the mountain, something else Hunter wouldn't expect. He'd think I was going to head down into town, maybe hoping to catch a ride along the way. But there was no hope for me in Addison. Not with Stepmama there. Instead I plunged into the deepest woods in the hopes that it would offer enough brush to hide me whenever I needed to lie down to catch my breath. If I could avoid Hunter for

. . . .

the next hour or two, the sun would set behind the mountain. I doubted he'd keep up a search for me after dark.

Unless he had hounds.

Hunters usually had hounds, didn't they? But then, his *name* was Hunter, not his work.

For a few minutes that thought comforted me, till I realized I didn't *know* if he had hounds. Or if he actually worked as a hunter. I didn't know *anything* about him, except that he had a knife and a bow and arrows and that he would do whatever Stepmama told him to do. He, too, was besot.

So I kept running. Running uphill, leaping logs, hurtling around tree trunks, sliding across muddy places, tripping over unseen tree roots, picking myself up off the ground and running again until I was out of breath and my sides hurt horribly.

Somewhere along the way, I lost one of my shoes. Somewhere I'd been hit on the left arm by a branch or briar, for there was blood running down toward my fingers. Somewhere . . . I didn't know where . . . there was a man trying to kill me for love.

For love of Stepmama, not for love of me.

"Think, Summer," I told myself, giving myself permission to stop when all I really wanted to do was to keep running.

. . . .

And so I stopped, thought, listened, hearing something loud nearby, as if a drummer had entered the woods and was sending signals to whoever was following me. It took me a moment before I realized it was only my own hard breathing and the drumbeat of my heart.

I can't go home. If I go home, Stepmama will kill me herself. Hunter all but said that. Poor Papa is on his own now.

Tears welled up for the first time, not for me and what I was going through, but for Papa. I hoped Cousin Nancy would look out for him.

As for me, my only chance was to get over the mountain, far enough away so that Hunter—even with dogs—couldn't find me. I was almost thirteen and strong for my age. Doing all those chores for Stepmama the past few years had toughened me. Maybe I could pass for older and find work.

But first I had to stay alive and out of Hunter's reach.

I ran.

Later that evening, too tired to move another step, I found a climbable oak and went up as far as I could manage in the dark. There, in the fork of the tree, I settled myself for the night. Yes, a bear could climb up if it wanted. But I hoped I was far enough up to discourage a bear from bothering me.

. . . .

There was a pair of owls singing back and forth for a while. *Maybe,* I thought, *maybe the white owl and its mate.* Though really, the soft *hoo-hoo-ho-ho-ho-hoooo* sounded more like a great horned owl.

A breeze rustled the leaves around me. It was already cold this far up on the mountain, and the breeze only made it colder. My thin dress didn't offer much warmth. But even so I fell asleep at once, the owl song almost a lullaby.

Sometime before dawn, I heard hounds baying quite far away, but near enough to be troubling. I supposed they could have been some men out jacking deer or hunting coons. The boys in our class had talked about such goings-on after Jimmy McGraw's papa took him out all night hunting and his mama had sent in a note excusing him from school on account of his needing his sleep. But just in case, I shinnied down that tree and headed on out, hoping to find running water. Dogs can't track you through running water. Bears nor painters neither.

When I found a stream, I took off my one shoe and waded in. My, that water was cold! Like sticking your feet in an icebox. But I stayed in it, going downstream as long as I could bear the cold before clambering up the other side. Along the way, I washed the blood off my arm and

. . . .

examined myself for ticks and scratches. I never heard the dogs again.

Was I hungry by then? Not so I noticed. But I was still tired and scared, a bad combination. It can make you careless. And the foot without the shoe seemed to find every stick and stone around. I lost track of the times I tripped and fell, banging one knee or the other.

I sat myself down for a moment to give myself a good scolding. "Summer," I said, though not aloud of course, "you need to be even more careful now." Because I'd no idea where I was. I could even have come in a big circle back near Hunter's trailer.

And I still didn't know if he had dogs.

The sun had risen up high enough that I could see it through the canopy of trees overhead, so I knew I was going east now. East would get me to Virginia and eventually the coast. I decided that would be my goal.

I kept to the shady forested areas, startling a doe and her fawn, who was all speckled and tiny. I stood still and watched them go, the mother far ahead and the baby wobbling after her.

Gray squirrels chittered out warnings from the trees. Crows followed me, scolding. A good hunter, even an ordinary hunter, would know from the noise where I was.

. . . .

But how could I stop squirrels and crows from giving me away?

Nervously, I brushed the hair out of my face and then thought about tying my hair back with the blue ribbon from around my waist. But when I reached down for it, it was gone.

Did I lose it early or late? I thought. *What if Hunter and his hounds found it? Or the lost shoe. Tracking me would be easier then.*

"Don't think about it," I whispered. "Keep going." And I kept on.

Now, in full daylight, I could see all around me, the trees no longer black trunks, but browns and grays and white. I noted oaks and pine and birch and others I couldn't name.

But if I could see the trees clearly, then *I* could be seen, too. So I stuck to a thicker part of the woods, skulking from tree to tree.

Skulking. Another book word I'd never said aloud before, but the perfect word for what I was doing.

Along the way I grabbed hold of a tree limb that had fallen off a big old oak. It might not scare away anything really dangerous, but it made me feel a lot safer, and that counted for something.

· · · · · · · · ·

I thought about eating. I hadn't had anything since lunch the day before and, judging by the sun, that was twenty-four hours earlier. Too soon in the spring for berries, and as I didn't trust harvesting mushrooms without someone who knew the bad ones from the good, I was worried there might not be anything for me to eat at all. My stomach growled.

Nobody ever died from a one day's fast, I told myself. So on I went.

Soon I came upon a small spring bubbling up into a marshy place, and that gave me an idea. I looked about for a patch of wild ramps somewhere on the tea-colored woodland floor. They love to have their feet in damp soil.

After about fifteen minutes of searching, I spotted a patch of the thin emerald-green leaves. Pulling up a bunch to expose about twenty small ramp bulbs, I dipped them into the pool to clean off the dirt that clung to them, then munched down a half dozen. Though I'd had ramps before—cut up in salads or fried up and served with rice— I'd never eaten a whole bunch of them raw. Very sharp and garlicky, but in the end quite filling. The rest I jammed into my pocket to eat later on. I knew that my breath would stink from them, but since there was no one around to smell me, I figured it didn't matter.

. . . .

Nearby I found some lamb's-quarters in a small clearing. We had plenty of that growing in our garden, and they are good to eat, cooked or raw, so I knew that would be safe. And close to, I found wild mint as well, which finished off my small meal and made my mouth taste fresh again.

Not exactly a hardy lunch, but enough to stop me from considering my belly every step of the way. Just as well. I had a lot more important things to think about: Hunter, dogs, bears, painters, Papa, and above all Stepmama.

By then it was mid-afternoon and I'd come to a large meadow with very few trees on either side. I sat down with my back against the last tree to consider what to do.

Be a fox, I told myself. *Be sly and thoughtful.* Foxes in the fairy tales could always out-think the other animals.

Walking straight across an open meadow in broad daylight seemed a crazy chance to take. Anyone might see me. So I melted back into the forest and climbed a tree to wait for nightfall. Or the sound of hounds. Whichever came first. And lucky I did because soon as I was settled on a branch, my legs wrapped around it for safety, my right hand over the caul bag for strength, I heard a woofing sound below me.

I moved slowly, quietly till I could see what was making the sound. A big black bear and her cub walked

· · · · · · · ·

right under the branches of my tree, heading toward the meadow. The woofing was the mother's way to get her baby to follow. And follow he did, though not without circling around her, running ahead, then frantically backtracking till he reached her side again. It was so funny, I almost laughed out loud.

Almost.

As they went across the meadow, they left a wide trail of crushed grass. I watched till they were long out of sight. Then I fell asleep, dreaming about bears all living together in a little cottage in the woods, with rocking chairs and beds and bowls full of tasty porridge.

When I woke, it was near dark. I made my way back to the edge of the meadow and realized that it was much larger than I'd first thought. But the bears had left such a huge path as they'd rambled across the high grass, I thought that it would make easy walking for me.

Before I stepped onto the trail, I had another thought: *If this is the bears' favorite path, I don't dare use it.* What if I bumped into them coming back home for the night? What if the baby bear was ahead and I cut him off from his mother? Then there'd be nowhere for me to run.

So instead, I kept edging around the meadow, hoping to find some other way across. It seemed like miles

· · · · · · · ·

and miles and miles to go, but I knew I'd taken the safer way.

Safe was good.

As things got darker, I could no longer tell which way east lay. I turned around and around, trying to figure it out. In the end, trying to be foxy, I'd outfoxed myself. I was more lost now than I'd been before.

I didn't dare wait until the next morning. By then anyone trailing me might find me. My only hope was to go forward, quickly.

So I faded back into the forest but near enough to the meadow that I would still have a bit of moonlight as a guide.

And that's when I saw the eerie glow coming from an old tree stump as if magic had set the woods aglow. The kind of magic a witch might do. At first I was startled, then frightened. If Stepmama had found me, all was truly lost.

But soon enough sense returned and I knew what I was seeing. Not magic at all.

Fox fire!

I stepped closer and there was a cluster of orange mushrooms, their undersides glowing a soft green. Oh, I knew these weren't for eating. Jack-o'-lantern mushrooms could make a person sick for days with stomach cramps and the runs. But I *could* follow them in the dark, going from cluster to cluster. My own private path.

· · · · · · · ·

"Thank you," I whispered, unclear this time who I was thanking.

So, all alone in the dark woods I followed the jack-o'-lanterns' glow till I was simply too tired to go any farther. Luckily, I found a hollow in a tree, too narrow for a bear but just right for me. It was warmer there than up on a tree limb. The breezes couldn't reach me and the heat I made just by breathing seemed to envelop me. I settled myself down for a nap that turned into a long, deep, healing sleep.

When morning came with a chorus of birdsong, I was ready to go on. After chowing down on half of the leftover ramp bulbs and rinsing my mouth with some water from a stream, I raced around the meadow and found myself on the eastern downslope of the mountain.

Am I safe? So far that day I'd heard no hounds, no bears, no cars or trucks, no gunshots. No crackle of footsteps on leaves or fallen branches behind me or ahead of me. So, safe enough.

I was almost giddy with relief.

Avoiding the patches of loose rocks as much for safety as for the noise, I stayed within the embrace of the trees on the way down. I passed by a cave like a yawning mouth and found myself suddenly on a well-worn path.

· · · · · · · ·

I wondered if I should avoid it, for fear of meeting someone. About to step off the path and plunge back into the undergrowth, I suddenly heard a growl behind me. A full-throated, angry growl. Looking over my shoulder, I saw a huge black bear standing up on its hind legs in front of the cave. It was staring down at me, jaws open and white drool forming in the corners of its mouth.

I don't think I screamed, but I must have because someone did. I started to run, knowing it was a stupid thing to do. But my mind couldn't control my legs. I raced down the path heedless of anything but the beast at my back. And it *was* at my back. I could hear its heavy breathing behind me.

Did I turn and look? Of course not. I was only intent on escape. And when, rounding a corner, I saw a strange little house at the edge of the next turning, standing like a triangle under a stand of pine trees, I cried aloud, sure I was saved.

A hot breath at my neck sighed with me. A bear sigh. I threw the stick I'd been holding over my shoulder and heard a satisfying *thunk* as it struck home. All I could hope for was that it would distract the bear for a second or two.

The hot breath on my neck disappeared.

· · · · · · · ·

I thought I'd outrun the bear.

I hadn't.

I thought the bear had let me go.

It hadn't.

In fact, the bear was shepherding me toward the house and I didn't know that's what it was doing until long after.

·24·

SEVEN BEDS

 reached the house. The door-knob turned. I flung the door open and slammed it closed behind me. I could feel the heavy thud as the bear hit the door a moment after.

My heart was chugging painfully in my chest at the close call. Frantically, I glanced around for something to prop up under the doorknob,

. . . .

something strong enough to keep the front door closed against the weight of that enormous fierce beast.

To my right stood a chair, high-backed and sturdy-looking, with a needlework seat. Afraid to move from the door, I managed to angle my foot around one of the chair's rungs and slide it over with my foot. Then I turned and quickly jammed it under the knob. It seemed to hold. But just in case, I looked about for a back door, somewhere I could use to escape if the bear broke in.

Across the crowded room, stuffed with sofas and chairs and a large table piled high with papers, I could see several doors. I chanced racing across.

One door led to a tidy kitchen, another to an inside privy. A third opened inward to a bedroom cluttered with seven beds. Six were on the small side, hardly larger than a child's bed. The seventh was regular-sized. If there was a mother or father here all alone with six small children, surely I could be of some help.

The six small beds were each neatly made up, with sheets, a pillow in a pillowcase, and a hand-pieced quilt. The largest bed had no bedding on it at all, only a handsome wedding-ring quilt folded at the bed foot. Everything was too neat for it to be a father and children. It had to be a mother. When they got home, I'd explain everything to them.

. . . .

But what if they came home to a house where a fierce bear lay in wait? Had I led them, poor mites, into a trap?

There were four windows against the far wall. I could use one of those for escape should I need to get out to warn the family.

Closing the bedroom door quietly behind me with a soft click so as not to alert the bear, I turned and put my ear to the door. I listened hard for any houghing or growling or heavy steps, anything to indicate the bear had gotten in.

The house was surprisingly quiet.

Too quiet.

I thought again about the mother and her children. What could I do? What should I do?

I pushed the big bed against the door to hold it shut before I felt in the slightest bit safe.

Then, curled up on the bed, I listened for about a half hour longer, straining to hear anything that could mean the bear had gotten in through the front door or the mother and children had returned home. After a time, I let my fear go and my exhaustion creep in. With the quilt held tight around me with my left hand, the caul bag even more tightly in my right, I closed my eyes. Before I knew it, I'd fallen asleep.

. . . .

•

When at last I awoke, it must have been hours later, for what I could see of sky through the window was late afternoon. There was a sound like someone at the front door, pushing it open: the chair falling on the floor and many great shouts.

Not a bear, then, I thought sleepily, but got no further with that thought, because suddenly the door to the bedroom starting moving inward, which meant the bed I was on was moving, too.

I heard men's voices, angry voices—three, four, five of them. They were cursing in some foreign tongue. Not children at all.

Had I fallen into a robber's den? Ali Baba and the thieves? A murderer's home like Bluebeard's castle? Had I escaped from one sure death into the path of another? *Frying pan into the fire,* Cousin Nancy would have said. I could all but feel the flames.

Throwing the quilt to one side and leaping off the bed, I raced to the bank of windows, now my only means of escape. I stood on the bed closest to the wall and pushed open a window. Clambering onto the sill, I stuck my feet out, readying myself to leap. I'd take my chances outside rather than be found here sleeping, like Goldilocks in the Three Bears' house.

· · · · · · · ·

The very thought of *three* bears made me shiver anew. One had been bad enough.

As I glanced over my shoulder, the door opened a crack and then was shoved wide, the bed squealing in protest as it slid along the floor. To my amazement, three rather small, wiry men stumbled in.

"Hold!" one of them called to me as I gathered myself to jump from the window ledge. He had, I noticed almost calmly, a long graying beard.

"Don't jump!" the second shouted.

"Cliff's edge!" That was the third little man.

Only then did I turn and look down. Just as the third had warned, a huge chasm yawned beneath my feet. From where I sat, I couldn't see the bottom of it. There was only about a foot between where I'd planned to jump down and the edge. If I'd leapt without knowing, I'd most probably have tumbled in and been dead from the fall.

But if I stayed . . .

I looked back at the men who'd called out the danger. Who no doubt had chased off the bear. Then I turned again and looked at the gulf below my feet. Clutching the caul bag, I measured one danger against another—an unknown frying pan against certain fire.

I stayed.

· · · · · · · ·

"Giff me your hand," said the man with the gray beard, coming closer.

"No one shall harm you," said the second. He was almost completely bald, his head shining like Mama's white teapot.

"Gott im Himmel," said the third, "it's a girl." He had reddish hair and flyaway eyebrows.

I looked at the three of them. For all that they differed in coloring, there was a sameness about them: same height, same broad shoulders, same sky blue eyes. Their voices didn't have the twang of a Webster County man's, and some of their words were strange, but they were comforting all the same.

I let myself fall back onto the bed, sat up, stood. But I gave no one my hand, all the while thinking about that strange phrase: *Gott im Himmel.* It sounded like no words I knew.

"Are you aliens?" I asked at last, thinking about the pictures of the odd creatures from outer space on the covers of Papa's paperback books.

"Aliens? *Ja.* Ve are miners from Hessen," said the graybeard.

All right, I thought, *I can deal with aliens.* After all, I'd already endured two years of a witch stepmother, encoun-

· · · · · · · ·

tered a snake-handling preacher, run from a knife-wielding hunter, and just now eluded a charging bear. How could I be afraid of these small creatures?

I held out my hand. "My name is Snow-in-Summer Morton," I said. "Welcome to West Virginia."

Unaccountably, the three of them began to laugh.

I folded up the wedding-ring quilt carefully and set it at the foot of the bed, while the little creatures nodded in an approving way. Baldy and Gott im Himmel moved the bed back to its rightful place. And Graybeard closed the window. Only then did they escort me into the living room, where three others were waiting, as small and as broad-shouldered and as blue-eyed as they. Graybeard showed me to a chair and then they all made a loose circle around me.

I suppose I should have been afraid, but they weren't scary at all. Even when they began questioning me, I felt instantly that they did it because they wanted to help.

"Vy are you here?" Graybeard asked.

"And look at you, poor child," added Baldy, "you're filthy. Vat a terrible time you must have had."

Their sweet concern broke down the wall around me and tears began to fill my eyes. I scrubbed at them with one fist, which only made things fuzzy.

· · · · · · · ·

Gott im Himmel offered me a large white handkerchief, rather the worse for wear. It had dark smudges on both sides, but then—I supposed—so did I. I took the handkerchief and dabbed at my eyes.

"Start from the start," Graybeard said softly.

"There's . . . there's an awful lot to tell." My voice was suddenly quite shaky. "And a lot of it is awful."

They laughed again.

"Ve haff quit vork for the day," Baldy said, "so ve haff much time for tales."

Gott im Himmel added, "And ve *luff* a good story."

"There's little good about it," I said.

Graybeard held a finger up. "Let us be the judge of that, child."

Nods ran all around the circle.

Then Graybeard introduced them all to me. He was Jakob, Baldy was Karl, Gott im Himmel was really Philip. Redbeard was Friedrich, called Freddy. The short one was Klaus. And the dark-bearded one was George. Hardly the kind of alien names in Papa's books. Which had too few consonants and a lot of apostrophes.

"Und how long since you've last eaten?" asked George.

I thought a minute. "Since yesterday morning? A bit of lamb's-quarters and a handful of ramps." I pulled the last

. . . .

couple of ramp bulbs out of my pocket. The leaves were broken and wilted, the bulbs crushed. A pungent garlic smell filled the air.

"Get the child some tea," Jakob ordered, and Klaus wandered off at once, I guessed going into the kitchen.

"Und some sausage and *küchen*," Freddy called after him.

"Thank you," I said, not knowing what *küchen* was but hoping it tasted good, though at that moment *anything* would have tasted good. Even more ramps.

The küchen turned out to be a little apple cake, very moist and sweet. And along with it came bread and butter, sausage, and mashed potatoes. A feast.

"Ve have only tea or beer or vater to drink," Jakob said. "Ve're not used to being visited by little girls."

"Little girls on the run," added Freddy with a shrewd guess.

"I'm not *so* little," I explained. Then, not wanting to be impolite, for I was taller than the six of them, I added quickly, "After all, I'm nearly thirteen. And I can shift for myself."

"So it seems." Jakob nodded with approval and I felt myself swell a bit with pride.

That's when I told them the whole story as I knew it, starting with Mama's death and going right up till that very moment. It took a better part of an hour in the telling, even

. . . .

though I left loads of it out. The bread and sausage and küchen kept me going, and the teapot seemed as endless as the cooking pot in the old fairy tale.

When I finished my story, Philip laughed. "Ursula knows her job."

I was confused. "Ursula?" I looked around. I'd seen no one who might be Ursula.

Seeing my confusion, Philip said, "The bear."

"The *bear*?"

"Yah," added Klaus, "she must have seen you needed help and shooed you into the house. Then she came and got us from the mine."

"The bear. Shooed. Me." I put a hand to my brow, stunned.

Freddy added, "Ve raised her from an orphan cub. She's the family pet."

"And our guardian, too," Karl added, raising a finger. "Don't forget that."

The others chuckled.

"Now that she has your scent and ours together, she'll be on the vatch for you, too," Jakob told me. "Just in case Stepmama . . ." He left the rest hanging, but I knew what he meant.

However, I told myself, *Stepmama will never think to look for me here, on the far side of Elk Mountain, in a small house, with a bunch of little men, and guarded by a bear!*

· · · · · · · ·

"Thank you," I said.

"*Bitte schön,*" said Philip.

He was right. It was a very *bitter* story.

Of course, once I was fed and safe, and fully delivered of my tale the way a mother is delivered of a difficult child, I realized how truly filthy I was. The little men—for now I thought of them that way, not aliens at all—drew out a metal tub from under the kitchen sink and heated up water in the kettle though it took some twenty kettles to fill it up to the top. Then they gave me three towels and a bar of pinkish soap.

"Ve make the soap ourselves," Klaus said shyly. "Smell it."

I took a long sniff. "Mint," I said. "Very fresh."

He was pleased I knew it. "And vakening," he said.

I thought I knew what he meant. The scent would wake me up.

They placed fresh clothes for me on a wooden rack near the bath.

"These were Mutti's clothes," George said. "Mama, you vould call her. She is no longer vith us. Perhaps they fit you."

"I know how to alter dresses," I said, for we'd learned that in home ec. "If you have a needle and thread."

"Ve haff even better—ve haff Mutti's sewing machine," he said. "Do you know how to use a treadle?"

· · · · · · · ·

I grinned. I learned that in home ec, too!

They gave me my choice of three outfits. My favorite was a sweet little red and white dress they called a dirndl that had a full skirt, gathered waist, and fitted bodice just my size. The other two were floral cottons, one with blue flowers, the other with yellow, and they were both just right, only needed a bit of hemming. Their *mutti* must have been tall, for all that they were tiny men.

"I think these are beautiful," I said, "but this one"—I pointed to the dirndl, not daring to touch it with my filthy hands— "is much too pretty for me to wear."

"Mutti vore it to church," said Jakob.

"Und venever there vas a music party," added George.

Karl sighed. "How Mutti loved to dance."

A music party! I tried to imagine such a thing and failed. I'd not been to a party that I could remember, except when Papa married Stepmama, in seven years or longer. But I was not here for a party.

"This one," I said, choosing the more sensible blue cotton dress.

"You vill look *wunderbar* in it, child," Jakob said. "But you need not choose. They can *all* be yours. Mutti needs them no more."

The little men had also set out some of Mutti's underthings on the rack, though they seemed ill at ease

· · · · · · · ·

handling them. They left a pair of their mother's shoes as well. Luckily, they fit me and that was a blessing since I'd no idea how to alter shoes. Especially not such sturdy brown leather shoes, which would be perfect for walking up and down mountains. All the way to Virginia.

"How long has your mama been gone?" I asked them.

"She died vhen Villy was born," said Jakob.

"Which of you is Villy?" I looked around. Then I put my hand over my mouth. What if Villy had died just as our baby had died and been buried with his dear mama?

"Villy is at the uniwersity," Jakob said. "He is learning philosophy."

"Und linguistics," Freddy added.

I didn't know what either of those things were but filed the words away in my mind to unpack later. But then I thought—if Villy was at the university, he must have been born at least eighteen years ago. More and more mysterious.

"He vill *not* be a miner like us. Ve promised Mutti," Freddy said.

"He's a true American," Klaus added. "Not born in the old country, but here in the big bed."

I wondered where the old country was, wondered about Villy, whether he was short like his brothers and bearded. Whether he had red hair or black hair or no hair at all.

"Do Mutti's clothes suit you?" Philip asked.

. . . .

"Oh, very much," I said.

"There is more then," Jakob said.

"*Much* more," added Freddy.

Thinking of the eighteen years, I asked: "You kept her clothes all this time?"

The nods went all around.

"You must have loved her very much." I smiled at them. "Just as I loved my mama, too, but I had so little time with her. Only seven years." I thought a minute. "What about your papa?"

"He died soon after. Of a broken heart."

"Ah," I said, nodding with understanding. I was thinking that my papa would have been the same if Stepmama hadn't put him under her wicked spell. And wasn't that odd, then, for in a way she'd saved him. I knew she hadn't meant to. I thought she'd be horrified if she knew. And *that* made me smile.

They went outside and waited for me to take my bath. I soaked for a long while, eyes closed. I could hear the men chatting away and smell the smoke of their pipes through an open window. I felt the dirt and the fear being washed away. As ever, my caul in its little bag lay close at hand . . . just in case.

. . . .

Opening my eyes, I got down to the hard business of giving myself a real scrub before the water went cold, soaping up my hair, then ducking under to rinse the soap out. At last I got out, smelling wonderfully minty. Drying myself thoroughly, I put on Mutti's blue cotton dress before calling the little men back inside. I could hem it later.

"If I can stay just a night or two, I'll get your house sparkling clean and then be on my way. I'm a good worker. Really I am. I did all the housework at my house." I smiled again at them. I think I'd smiled more in those first few hours with them than I had in the last six years. "You seem to have an extra bed . . ."

"Ve'll move it into the music room," Karl said.

"But vere vill Villy sleep?" Freddy looked troubled.

Jakob smiled. "He is not due back from uniwersity till sometime next month. Und he can alvays stay on the couch if Summer is still here."

"Oh," I said, looking around at the cozy, comfortable cottage with a bit of regret. Already I knew I'd miss these gentle little men. "I'll be long gone by then."

· · · · · · · ·

·25·

STEPMAMA REMEMBERS

f the mirror said she was lost, then she wasn't dead. At least, not yet. I was shaking with fury, but by the time I'd gotten to the car, I was coldly in control.

The mirror can't lie.

But a man can.

I drove up the mountains paying no attention to the speed, just set on confronting that stupid Hunter. I'd given him one thing to do for me, a day and a night to accomplish

. . . .

it, and clearly he'd not done it. Perhaps he'd taken pity on Snow, was holding her captive. Perhaps he'd fallen for her innocence. Whatever he'd done, it wasn't what I asked. I floored the gas pedal and the trees seemed to blur on either side as I raced along the road.

When I turned into his drive, he was sitting on his front step throwing a knife into the ground over and over and over again. Mumblety-peg. A boy's game.

I got out of the car and walked over to him, my shoulders squared. It would have been better if I smiled at him, to put him at ease. But I could not.

He glanced up, something like fear and something like pleasure mixing on his face, looking for all the world like a pup who's just messed on the floor and expected to be hit with the rolled newspaper but hoping the tail wag would still work its magic. He had a deep scratch near one eye.

Standing, he said, "Ma'am, I was just thinking about you."

I was sure he had been. I asked, "Did you do what we agreed to?"

The tail wagging slowed, stopped. He looked at me, trying to replace fear with innocence. It didn't work. "Yes, ma'am. Cut out her heart, stewed it like you said, and ate it, too." He licked his lips, whether from playacting or fright

. . . .

wasn't clear. But that fabulation was too much over the top, and even he knew it. He couldn't meet my eyes.

"Did she run off or did you just leave her in the woods hoping that would do instead?" I crossed my arms and waited for his answer.

He stared down at his shoes for a long moment, then made a small shrug with his shoulders before looking up again, trying once more for innocence though this time it looked incredibly like stupidity crossed with ineptitude. "I *did* what you said." There was a hint of surliness.

"You did not."

"Who says that? How could anyone know . . ."

I almost growled at him but didn't change my stance. "*I* know. And that's enough."

"Well, gone's gone," he said, shrugging. He tried to smile. "She's well and truly lost. I tracked her far up onto the mountain. There was bear scat and mountain lion spoor. She's a juicy one. She won't have lasted the night."

"She'd better *stay* lost," I said, reaching into my tote bag and hauling out a bottle of moonshine.

"What's this?" He looked curious, then fearful, then curious again.

I thought: This *is what comes of asking a boy to do a man's job*. I smiled at him beguilingly, but all the while I was

· · · · · · · ·

thinking: *The preacher was useless, and Hunter even worse. At least I don't have to listen to those stupid sermons anymore.* My smile got broader.

He wanted the smile to be true, wanted *me* to be true, and so he was easily convinced. "This is just the start of the payment?"

I made my smile look more sincere. I should have been in the movies. Greta Garbo, maybe. Joan Fontaine. I still could be, once I got the money for the land. Who needs a girl to be my apprentice, my poppet, my shadow? Who needs this particular difficult one to drain her of essence? I'd already waited too long and she'd gone and become a woman before I was ready. There would be plenty and more willing girls once I became a movie star.

I ran my fingernails along the back of Hunter's hand, finding another scratch there. Probably from the girl. "Just the start," I cooed, moving to embrace him. I could feel a year of his young, brute strength flow into me. But too much of his stupidity came with it, so I broke the connection. "We will have time for that later. First let's drink."

He took the bottle from me. "You're not mad at me."

"Gone is gone," I whispered, shrugged, still smiling.

We walked into his house and he got out two glasses. Then he opened the bottle, poured us each a drink. He

. . . .

downed his quickly and had poured another before I even lifted the glass to my lips. I'd known he'd drink that way, one quick one and then a second with me. Young men never know how to prolong a conversation—or anything else. I clinked my glass against his.

Then I watched as he lost consciousness, his face befuddled, hurt, and slack. I gathered him in my arms and took the rest of his short life while he died. Then I walked away, but didn't take the bottle with me. It was strychnine from the church. The police chief will figure it out, even if I have to help him do it. I didn't use one of my own concoctions. I hate to waste a good potion on stupidity.

As I got in the car, I looked back at that pitiful trailer.

"Gone is gone," I whispered. This time when I smiled, it was for real.

I knew that the mirror would tell me where to look for Snow. Oh, not straight out. Mirror magic never works in such a straightforward way.

I came into the house, brewed up a special herbal drink for Lem to keep him extra quiet for the next few hours, then went into my bedroom and locked the door behind.

Sitting down at the table, I twitched the drape off the mirror, drumming my fingers on the tabletop till the clouds parted and the dark mask swam into view.

. . . .

"Mirror, where is she?" I started to say, then realized I needed to slow down and ask the question as clearly, as specifically as I could.

"Where is the girl Snow in Summer now?"

The mask turned its empty eyes toward me. For a moment it looked as if it was laughing at me. Or snarling. With the mask it's difficult to tell.

"I'm sorry," I said, "for breaking the glass." The words pushed against my teeth as if trying to shatter them. I wasn't truly sorry, just annoyed, but tried to keep the annoyance out of my voice.

The mirror replied:

> *"She lives with six small men who mine,*
> *And a seventh she will know in time."*

"That's not even a good rhyme," I said. But it was enough. I *will* find her from what the mirror told me. Because though women lie when they have to and men lie all the time, the mirror always tells the truth.

Always.

·26·

A KNOCK AT THE DOOR

told the brothers to let me do the washing up from our meal, though they insisted on clearing away the dishes first. I commandeered their little sink, pumping the fresh water until it gushed freely. Though Papa's house had taps, some of the Morton cousins only had pumps like the brothers had, so I knew what must be done.

After the sink was filled with the cold water, I pumped some more into the kettle and heated it up. Then with the

· · · · · · · ·

hot water I scrubbed the plates and teacups till everything shone, rinsing them thoroughly in the cold.

Meanwhile, the brothers went into the music room, where I was now to sleep, and brought out their instruments. Jakob and Klaus played fiddles, Philip and Freddy took turns on the sole accordion, Karl played the harmonium, and George kept them all in time with his big bass drum.

While I worked, they made a merry sound. So for the first time since Papa stopped playing his banjo for me, I had tunes to accompany my chores. I was able to laugh out loud and sing along with them, though I actually knew only one or two of the tunes they played.

And so I stayed in the little house near the mine entrance, alongside the chasm, one happy day merging into the next. I promised myself—and them—that I would leave soon. But I stayed. And stayed. And stayed. Happiness makes even the worst dangers seem far away.

Each morning the brothers went off to the mine, where they dug not for coal like most of the miners in Webster County, but for rough jewels like garnets, amethysts, even the occasional ruby and emerald. These they polished at home and then Jakob—with one of the other brothers—would take their finds every few weeks to sell to jewelers in Charleston or Morgantown or Clarksburg.

· · · · · · · ·

And me? At first I filled my days with cleaning the house and sewing missing buttons back on their trousers. I hemmed up Mutti's dresses to fit me. But that took such a small part of my day. Of course after I discovered Willy's library tucked away in the closet of the music room—with his name neatly spelled out, both *Wilhelm* and *Willy* in a neat and careful hand—I began to read again, reading every book he had in English. The brothers read, too, though much of it was in a foreign language—German, as it turned out, not alien at all.

When I'd run through all of Willy's books, I managed to persuade Jakob to find me some other books, from a secondhand bookstore, when he next went on a selling trip.

"Especially fairy tales," I told him. "Do you know what I mean—fairy tales?"

He laughed. His laughter was like a big man's—full and deep and generous. "Have you heard of the Brothers Grimm?"

I nodded. "Of course."

"Vell, they vere Germans from Hessen, as are ve."

I laughed back. "But not miners."

"Not miners," he agreed. "But in Hessen, little Summer, there are more miners than there are fairy-tale makers."

"Here in West Virginia, too," I said, "though they mostly mine coal."

· · · · · · · ·

As he started out the door, I remembered the thing I'd meant to ask for and had forgotten. "And please also bring back packets of seeds." I gave him a list I'd made. "I'm going to plant you a garden."

Over a month had gone by, and though I kept meaning to leave, I stayed, one happy, fear-free day melting into the next.

The brothers, though, were more mindful of danger and warned me never to open the door to a stranger in case Stepmama or Hunter came by. As there had been no sign of either, I felt completely safe both in the house and outside of it as well. Inside I had locks on all the doors. Outside I had Ursula. She long ago had forgiven me for tossing the stick at her and now followed me around like a dog. A *big* dog.

Did I spare a thought for Papa and Cousin Nancy? I confess they were not at the top of my waking mind. But each night, before sleep, I worried about them and prayed for them till sleep overtook me. My dreams were all green.

Ursula was my constant companion whenever I went out into the woods to search for ramps or lamb's-quarter or dandelions and other things in nature's larder. She followed closely at my heels. And while I gathered any wild greens, stuffing them into my tote bag, she lay down

· · · · · · · ·

by me and kept a watch. Also she had a nose like a pig for truffles, finding edible plants and mushrooms growing up on tree trunks as well as any honey hives within a mile of the house.

I started the brothers' garden on the far side of their cottage, away from the chasm, planting vegetables and flowers, which I knew would be in full bloom even after I was gone. They'd never planted a garden for themselves though I'd found the remains of one.

"Mutti had a garden," Klaus explained. "It vas her pride and joy. She never allowed us in it, not to plant nor to reap."

Jakob had laughed at that explanation. "Voman's vork!" he said. "We hadn't time to care for it after she died." He took a deep breath. "Or the heart."

I shook my head. "So I suppose instead, you buy food in the cities and cart it back here whenever you're on your jewel trips. So much money spent. And the food all over-ripe or underdone." Papa would have said the same.

Philip held a hand up and tutted at me. "Ve hunt for the pot—grouse and duck and boar."

"I fish," Freddy added. "Brown trout. Yum."

"He fishes more than he catches," said Karl.

I laughed. Their little spats were always in fun. There was no malice in them. "Growing your own food makes for better eating," I told them, repeating what I'd learned in home ec class. "And better for you." I grinned. "Makes you grow big and strong."

"Vell, strong perhaps," said Freddy.

At that we all howled with laughter.

While I didn't have Papa's perfect gift with green things, I was miles better than the brothers, except for Klaus, who spent every evening after he got back from the mine by my side, learning all he could about gardening. It turned out he had green fingers like Papa's, if not quite as practiced.

That pleased me because I knew that even long after I'd left them, my little men would have something to remember me by.

I got Freddy, Karl, and Philip to put in a fence around the garden to keep it safe from marauding animals though really, we hardly needed it. With Ursula sleeping by the garden at night, we'd no trouble with pests like rabbits, groundhogs, moles, or deer. She'd marked her territory pretty well, and none of them dared come near.

Was I happy?

Never happier.

But happiness can breed complacency, a word that means "smug satisfaction," or "being unaware of danger." I relaxed too much into my new life, believing myself completely safe when, in fact, there was nothing safe about it at all.

It was just days before Willy was to come home from the university for the summer. And it was a week before I'd promised myself I would definitely be off east, heading toward Virginia. I was working as usual out in the side garden. It was so hot under the brilliant sun that I'd tied my hair back under one of Mutti's colorful scarves and had even taken off the caul bag, shoving it into the pocket of my shirt so it wouldn't lie heavily on my chest, making me sweat puddles.

As I bent over the carefully dug rows, disguised by the high grasses outside of the fence, I was all but invisible to any passersby. Though of course no one ever did pass by.

Ursula dozed by the foot of a nearby birch, quite stuffed with honeycomb that she'd discovered somewhere down the road. She'd brought a bit home as well for the brothers and me, and I'd already stored it in a canning jar. The brothers loved a teaspoon of honey in their porridge bowls.

My hands were in the dark soil, transplanting some lamb's-quarters I'd found back in the woods. Lamb's-

· · · · · · · ·

quarters—which the brothers called goosefoot—will take over a garden if you're not careful. But there's nothing better in salads, as Papa used to say, or steaming it to serve just like spinach. The peas and beans I'd planted were just starting up. Carrots and potatoes, too, their little green shoots pushing through the rich earth. Next I was going to plant the precious squash seeds Jakob had brought back for me. I planned ten hills of them. I'd already explained how they grew to Klaus, who wrote it all down in a little notebook because the root vegetables and the squash would be ready for harvest after I was gone.

Suddenly, breaking through my garden thoughts, I heard a knock at the front door and a crackling old voice called out, "Anybody home?"

Ursula was awake in an instant and began a low, rumbling growl. She began to stand, but I put a hand on her shoulder to keep her still.

"That doesn't sound like anyone I know," I whispered to her. "Not Stepmama nor Hunter. But we will be careful nonetheless."

Standing, I tried to tidy myself, wiping a dirt-encrusted hand across my forehead because my brow was sweaty. I was in my work clothes, not one of Mutti's nice dresses—a pair of Willy's old outgrown trousers and one of his shirts

· · · · · · · ·

tied up in front, which had become my regular gardening outfit. With the strings of the caul bag hanging out of the pocket of the shirt, I must have been quite a sight.

An old woman stood at the door. If I looked bad, she looked ten times worse. Her skin was like parchment stretched over brittle bones. Her hair, gray and greasy, hung down to her shoulders. Long, scraggly bangs almost obscured her eyes, which was just as well since the left had a white cast over it. Her cheeks were deeply sunken; hunger must have been a constant companion. A filthy dress and coat seemed to droop from her stooped shoulders as if from a hanger. Even if the dress and coat had been clean, they wouldn't have had any color, for years of washing had bleached them both to a uniform gray. Her shoes were broken; the left one had toes showing through and the right heel was half off.

If I looked like a disaster barely avoided, she looked like the disaster had hit her head-on. Poor woman.

It didn't occur to me to ask why she'd come this far up the mountain. She seemed so exhausted, with a pack on her back and a covered willow-weave basket over her left arm, that all I felt was pity, not blame.

"Grandma," I said to her, "how long since you've last eaten?" Just as the brothers had asked me.

She put a hand over her breast as if her heart hurt. "I . . . I can't rightly remember." Her voice creaked with age.

· · · · · · · ·

"Well, let me bring you out some tea and küchen." Even though she looked as if what she needed first was a good wash and a lie down, I'd promised the brothers I'd never let anyone into the house. They said it wasn't safe. And I'm always good as my word.

I led her by the trembling arm to the bench by the door. "Sit here, ma'am, and I'll bring you out something to eat. But don't bolt it, mind, it's quite rich food. Wouldn't want to risk you getting sick on it."

"You're a good child," she said, her crabbed fingers patting my hand.

Then I went inside.

I'd no sooner got to the kitchen than I heard footsteps at the door and I turned. She must have been bewildered or perhaps hard of hearing as well as half blind, for she'd tracked after me and she was standing at the door and holding on to the doorjamb as if ready to faint.

I stood there with the pan holding the freshly baked küchen in my hand, the kettle on the boil behind me, and made a decision. "Oh, you poor thing," I said. "Sit here at the table before you fall over."

She was in the house and already had the pack off her back, the basket held toward me, before I'd finished speaking.

"Thank you, dear child," she quavered. "And you must take this as a gift from me for your sweet invitation."

· · · · · · · ·

I didn't have the heart to send her back outside into the hot sun now that she was already in the house. It would have been ungracious. And I feared that if I refused her offering, whatever it was, I'd surely hurt her pride. So I swallowed back an exasperated sigh and put out my hand for her gift.

·27·

COUSIN NANCY REMEMBERS

ach night after Summer had gone missing, I got down on my knees and prayed. And each morning before opening the post office, I went to church for confession. Father O'Hare looked annoyed to see me again, entering his side of the confessional with a heavy sigh. I knew he was tired of hearing me say the same thing. But I never stopped praying. Or confessing.

Never.

· · · · · · · ·

Else how would I ever be able to explain it to Ada Mae when we met in heaven? Church doctrine aside, I just knew that's where she and that precious baby boy were.

As for where Summer was, well, I refused to believe that she was in heaven with them. Not yet. I would have known it in my heart. I would have felt the pain of it under my breastbone. No, not dead, but surely taken, probably hurt, terrified, beaten down, confined. I couldn't think enough bad thoughts, which the priest dismissed by giving me some Our Fathers and Hail Marys, more and more each day.

When Charlie Hatfield finally got around to asking Step-mama in the second week that Summer was gone, the witch said she'd run off with a boy she'd met at church; she didn't rightly know his name. And that of course she'd hired a private detective to find them and bring them back though she didn't offer up his name and number.

"But if they've gone and gotten married," she said in a tight voice, "I expect Snow is no different than her mother, Ada Mae."

In that way, she condemned both of them in a single breath, which to me meant she was condemning herself.

And silly old Charlie Hatfield fell under her spell even as she spoke, and didn't do anything more about it except

· · · · · · · ·

send around notices to the towns closest to us to be on the lookout for a girl in a blue dress.

No amount of my telling Charlie that Summer wasn't the kind of girl to run off with a boy she just met made an ounce of difference. He was set on believing the witch.

"And don't you come around here with your fairy stories anymore, Nan," he said to me, wagging his finger at me as if he was my pa instead of the little old fat boy in our class who'd never had a single friend because he was a squealer and mean besides.

And that was that, except for my prayers, till a man out walking his dog on the far side of Elk Mountain found a torn piece of Summer's blue dress and the ribbon that had been about her waist. They were in a meadow overrun with bear tracks and fresh scat, and much too far from any town for her to have gotten there by any means other than bad business. Though by then—since it had been raining for days—the trail had gone cold. And even a pair of prize bloodhounds brought in from Buckhannon couldn't find Summer's scent.

· · · · · · · ·

·28·

DARKNESS DESCENDS

he basket was heavier than I expected. And something inside seemed to move about, making a funny buzzing noise. For a moment, I was afraid. But just a moment.

"What's inside the basket, ma'am?" I asked.

"I make little figures that walk about by clockwork," she said, scissoring a walking motion with her two pointer

• • • • • • • •

fingers. "I sell them door-to-door. It keeps body and soul together."

"Oh, like our clock." I pointed to the clock on the wall. Every hour a little clockwork bird came out of a hole singing. The first time I heard it, I was startled, but now I loved to listen to its little song. "The brothers brought it from the old country."

She looked sharply at me with her one good eye. "Brothers? Where are they now?" Her voice suddenly sounded stronger.

"In the mines." I set the basket down on the table. We could look at her clockwork figures after she'd been fed. I'd take one as a gift, even offer to buy it from her with money the brothers had been setting aside in a tin box over the sink for when I went on my way. After that, I'd send her off. There was something about her that made me uneasy, but not uneasy enough to forget my manners. But go she would have to, before the brothers came home for their dinner, found her in the house, and scolded me for letting her in.

I cut a slice of the küchen for her and one for me. She took it gratefully and crammed half of it in her mouth at once, as if eager to be getting on.

I brewed the tea and she washed the second half of the küchen down with that.

. . . .

"Thank you, dearie. So delicious," she said. "Did you make it yourself?"

I nodded. Klaus had shown me how.

The old woman stood. "Now pick out your present, and I will let you be."

I was somehow suddenly shy, almost reluctant to let her go, the first person other than the brothers I'd spoken to in over a month. But I set that feeling aside because it was more important for both of us that she be gone. Picking up the basket, I propped it in my left arm and lifted the lid.

The buzzing sound was so loud, I looked in, and there glaring up at me was the largest rattler I'd seen outside of the With Signs church.

I cried out and dropped the basket as the old woman laughed. Looking up, I saw that she'd ripped the white cast from her bad eye and was now staring at me, her one blue eye and one green eye as venomous-looking as the snake's, and both full of laughter.

"Stepmama!" I cried, and at the same time felt something sharp pierce my ankle. Horrified, I looked down. I'd been struck by the rattler.

She laughed, her voice high and crazed. "The mirror gave you away, child. It said:

. . . .

'She lives with six small men who mine,
And a seventh she will know in time.'

"It did not take more than a month and a bit of asking around to find you. What Hunter could not do, I surely can. He served me ill and found his doom. The snake has mostly been milked, but there will be enough venom to keep you under and I will take you from here and suck your essence before you die. It would have been better had you given it willingly. But in a few days your essence will be mine. My youth restored. And then the father. And the land. All three. The charm," she cried out wildly, "the charm's wound up."

Laughing, she came toward me, hands stretched out. I was suddenly terrified to let her touch me, even more than I was afraid of the snake at my foot, so I took the caul out of my shirt pocket, stripped it out of the bag, and flung it in her face. Where it hit her, fire burst forth and seared her blue eye and her ancient face melted like candle wax into a semblance of the Step-mama I knew.

She screamed, and as she screamed I picked up the frying pan from the table where I'd left it. It was suddenly heavy as a stone, heavy as doom. I had to use two hands

. . . .

but managed to bring it around in front of me, slamming it down again and again on the top of the snake till it let go of my ankle, till it stopped moving, till it was squashed under the heavy iron skillet.

Dead.

Dead as I would surely be in a minute.

In an hour.

By day's end.

I sank to the floor, feeling the poison move up my leg, burning beneath the skin. Death's arrow, death's lance, death's river flowing up my veins, seeking my heart.

I lay down, sweating, not with fear, no longer with fear, but with the poison.

Dark descended, though I knew it was day.

I couldn't see, but I could still hear.

I could hear Stepmama still screaming, but quieter now, almost a whimper.

I could hear Ursula at the door, growling and shaking something beneath her mighty paws and teeth.

I heard a voice I didn't recognize shouting, "Drop her! Drop her, you silly bear."

I heard the little men greeting someone. I heard their familiar, comforting voices: Jakob and Freddy and Karl

. . . .

and Klaus, Philip and George. Their voices came closer, surrounding me with their concern.

I tried to speak, but my voice was weak, even to my own ears. I tried again. "Papa," I said. "Tell Papa he's free."

And then I heard nothing more.

· · · · · · · ·

·29·

JAKOB REMEMBERS

e buried her at the crossroads below the house at midnight as deep as ve could, a stake in her heart. Best no one ever finds her and asks questions. Ve were all vitness to the final deed, all seven of us. Brothers, you know, stick together.

And then ve had to clean the house up. Vhat a mess ve had found on returning home. Klaus had gone early to help

. . . .

Summer vith the garden and came running back screaming for us to get out, get out and come right away.

The terror in his woice conwinced us and ve dropped tools and ran. Ve were only minutes away, of course, but it seemed as if it took hours to get there. Vhen ve arrived, ve found a mass of old clothes by the door, vith Ursula still worrying it. Only later did ve realize it was the remains of a voman, hideously battered as if vith a frying pan.

Villy had come home to this scene of horror and vas bending over Summer, still in her gardening clothes, in a svoon on the floor. His mouth vas on her ankle.

"Vat is he doing?" I shouted, then saw the dead snake on the floor and knew. He'd made a cross vith his knife over the point vhere the poison had gone in and vas sucking out as much of it as he could.

Klaus vas standing over him, veeping. "Too late. Too late."

And indeed it looked far too late, for Summer vas pale as death, her face vhite vith that black hair spread out and a trickle of red blood at her mouth. Vhite and black and red.

Her ankle vhere the snake had bitten it vas svollen. Not a lot, not black already, vhich vould have been for the vorst, but you could see how it vas much puffier than the other ankle.

. . . .

"Is this Summer, the one you wrote me about?" Villy asked.

I nodded.

"She's too young, too beautiful to die like this," he said. "I can't allow it." He bent back to suck out more of the poison.

But ve both knew that death can come at any age, come as vell to the young and beautiful as the old and vretched. Our mother had died in the prime of her life, in this wery house, giving birth to him.

"Young and beautiful," I said, "and good, too."

He did not again stop his awful task.

"But Villy, only God allows and disallows."

Philip began saying a prayer over Summer, but Villy sat back, then bent down and picked something up off of the ground, something gray and rubbery-looking, like a little cap.

"That must be the caul she told us about," Freddy said. "In her story."

"Her *story*," I said. "Ve thought it just a fairy tale, really. A young girl running away from home because of a vicked stepmother. The Brüder Grimm could have vritten it. And then she showed us the caul bag she vore around her neck."

. . . .

238

Freddy found the bag not far from vhere Summer lay. He put the caul back in the bag. Gave it to me. I placed it around Summer's neck.

And then something unexpected happened. Summer sighed. Opened one eye, closed it again. She vhispered something. Villy, who was closest, vas the only one who heard vhat she said.

"She says to tell her papa he's free," he reported.

"She's not dead yet," I said. "Ve need to get her to a doctor."

Villy shook his head. "She shouldn't be moved. It'll only make the poison go faster. You have to get a doctor to come here."

Freddy and Philip raced down the road, vhile Klaus and Karl moved the old voman's body to the mine for safekeeping till ve had time to figure out vhat to do vith it. They left Ursula to guard the mine entrance.

Meanvhile, Villy, George, and I piled blankets on Summer to keep her varm. Then ve took turns sitting by her side till the doctor arrived with some tventy wials of anti-wenom.

To his great surprise, after using only six, Summer vas suddenly avake and talking.

· · · · · · · ·

The doctor said he vas amazed but took her to the hospital anyvays. She vas there for more than a month, because there vere other problems that the wenom caused and they needed to keep a close eye on her.

All the vhile Villy sat vith her, talked to her, read to her, hardly left her side.

Her father and her cousin Nancy came from Addison two veeks into Summer's treatment. He vas a handsome man, somewhat vorn down from his years with the vitch. And Cousin Nancy vas a modestly handsome voman. She held Summer's hand, but her papa vept vhen he saw the girl lying in the hospital bed.

"Don't cry, Papa, the doctor says I will be fine. Just some scars. Willy says it makes me more interesting than merely being pretty." She laughed. "Imagine me, pretty."

"Pretty as a summer's day," said her papa. "Always was. Always will be. The spit of your mama."

"Amen to that," Cousin Nancy said. A truly good voman, as I came to find out.

. . . .

PHOTOGRAPH

he photograph of our wedding is in color. We are standing in front of the church up the mountain so Mama can be part of the ceremony, too. Cousin Nancy got special dispensation to attend from Father Clarke, the new priest.

It is my nineteenth birthday, so we are celebrating that as well as the wedding. The church has been filled with wildflowers cut from the mountainside. I insisted on them.

· · · · · · · ·

In the picture I am in a long white dress that I sewed myself on Mutti's sewing machine, with sparkling white jewels Jakob had bought in Clarksburg encrusting the bodice. I am wearing a wedding crown that had belonged to Mutti and a necklace that had been Mama's. Cousin Nancy had given me a lace handkerchief sewn on all sides with blue stitching, which I tucked into my sleeve.

"Though I hope you never use it to cry with," she said.

"The crying days are over," I told her. And indeed they are.

My hair is long and down to my waist and I look much younger than nineteen, but I think it's the combination of happiness and astonishment.

To one side of us stand Papa and Cousin Nancy, shyly holding hands. They have only just decided that they will get married, too, a quiet ceremony at Christmas when Willy and I will be home for the holidays. Father Clarke will officiate.

To the other side are the six brothers. Jakob looks like a proud papa though he's just eighteen years older than Willy. George stares at his feet but is smiling. Naughty Freddy is making rabbit ears behind Jakob's head while Karl and Klaus look at each other, mouths open, as if sharing a secret. Only Philip is staring directly at the camera.

. . . .

They have left Ursula at home. Or so they think. But if you look very carefully in the churchyard behind us, near Mama's grave, you can see a tuft of one ear above the gravestone and a bit of her behind. Above her, on the branch of a birch tree, wings stretched out as if it has just landed, perches a white owl. If you close your right eye and look at it with your left, it looks like a lady angel, her face framed by long dark hair and with a dimple in her chin.

As for me, I am gazing up at Willy, who has just begun his teaching at Wheeling College after three years of graduate school. He is in his one good suit, a dark blue that only emphasizes how slim he is. His round glasses perch on his nose as if they are about to fly off, which they often do. He's not smiling but looking quite serious because—as he said later—until we were off on our honeymoon and away from the churchyard, he wouldn't believe we'd really managed to get married after six years of courting.

But I always knew it would happen. After all, it was True Love from the very first moment we met. The best kind, born out of adversity and hard work and destined to last happily ever after. Of that we are both absolutely certain.

. . . .